MW00413639

BY: D. K. POSNER

REMY

First Edition

ISBN: 978-1-66782-709-4 (paperback)
ISBN: 978-1-66782-710-0 (ebook)

Publisher's Note: This book is a work of fiction. Any references to actual events or real people, living or dead, is entirely coincidental and are used fictitiously. Other names, characters, places, and events are products of the author's imagination, and any resemblance to actual events or places or persons, living or dead is entirely coincidental.

Author's website: https://dkposner.com
Facebook Author Page: fb.me/dkposner

Editing by Laura Hoffman
Cover Design by Lauren Darr

Published in the United States

For my children, my grandchildren, and

all who dream…

"I *have* to figure out a way…" Jonathon growled out the frustrated words while sitting at his desk staring at his computer in the solitude of his quiet upstairs bedroom in the old Victorian home where he grew up. With his elbows resting on each side of the keyboard and hands supporting the weight of his head, he began massaging his forehead, contemplating what to do about his current dilemma.

Until now, he always used his book smarts or familiarity with technology to give him answers. But this time he is in uncharted waters.

"Why do I care if she notices me!?" He grabbed a small lock of his hair, twisting it around his index finger, giving it a frustrated tug as he sat envisioning his beautiful classmate with her hunk of a boyfriend. Shoving away from his desk, he kicks the wall. His foot catches the electrical cord, and he scrambles to prevent his laptop and other items from toppling to the ground. Irritated even more by his clumsiness, he grits his teeth while letting out a barely audible groan. He wouldn't want his parents to overhear.

His entire 15 ¾ years, Jonathon Ewing Samuels III lived up to his family's distinguished name in every aspect. Brilliant to the point of being a little nerdy, he was always well-mannered and upstanding, often attending social events with his father and mother who were both well accomplished in the field of aerospace engineering. He would sit quietly nearby, scrolling through his phone as he eavesdropped on grown-up discussions of world events and politics at the private golf club where his parents belonged. Occasionally, he sipped tea with his mother's friends at charity events while she worked the room for donors benefitting scientific research. "Cheers," he often toasted them with his cup, sending them into bits of delighted laughter. Jonathon grew up to be, in his way, savoir faire.

Most parents anticipate the conflicting teenage years, but Mr. and Mrs. Samuels had no reason to believe their Jonathon wouldn't stay focused and aligned. And Jonathon was sincerely trying. However, recently he had become so captivated with his alluring classmate, his every waking hour was spent trying to figure out how to win her affection. Having no experience with girls, the logical solution (to Jonathon) was to turn to what he knew best, technology. Soon, he would create a clever invention to help him. And a few careless, desperate measures would land him in hot water with his best friend. But right now, he didn't know about the chaos to come or about the lessons he would learn.

Jonathon got up to open a window in his bedroom to let in some fresh air. He sat back down and began scrolling through his photos on his phone to find the one and only picture he had of Leana Parker. He'd taken it from across the counter when she had been intensely concentrating on a chemistry lab project and hadn't noticed him. She seldom paid *any* attention to him. And this was the problem he wanted to fix.

Leana, already 16, had wavy locks of chestnut brown hair nearly reaching her waist, usually neatly pulled back in a simple headband to match her outfit. In the one class they shared, Jonathon usually managed to inconspicuously get a seat near her. He thought she smelled like cinnamon and her perfectly milky-white complexion made him long to reach out to brush back a loose lock of hair just so he could graze her cheek with the back of his hand. He loved the sound of her voice and often fantasized talking privately with her, trying to make her giggle as he gazed into her chocolate brown eyes.

Although she and Jonathon had become friendly while working together during lab sessions, the object of her affection was a 6', 180 lb. junior who was part of the Varsity baseball team. He was strong enough to carry all six of her textbooks, plus his own AND his packed baseball bag at the same time. Not that he did this, but the fact he could made Jonathon feel slightly disadvantaged. Worse, the guy even had a more indomitable name than his own, Julius Rockefeller. Jonathon heard his nickname was Rocky on the baseball team but most of his friends called him JR, including Leana.

Frustrated again at the thoughts of his nemesis, Jonathon kicked the wall a second time, careful to avoid the cord this time but stubbing his big toe instead. "Great!" he muttered as he grabbed his foot to rub away the pain. Then he slouched over his desk and let his mind wander. He recalled the first time he noticed Leana and

JR in the hall chatting, and the pit in his stomach when he saw they were holding hands, realizing they were an item.

Sitting up again, Jonathon clinched both of his fists and flexed his biceps. Looking down at his arms reminded him he was no competition to JR's athletic abilities. Though his father had taken him to the golf range a few times, and he occasionally stepped into a pick-up game of tennis when one of his parents' friends had had too much scotch and couldn't play, Jonathon was more excited with non-physical competition. He enjoyed cheering on his school's Robotics Team but never joined as he was much too busy holding a lead seat on the school's Debate Team, despite being the youngest member.

When Jonathon looked in the mirror, he saw a boy turning into a young man before his eyes. Sparse stubble growing from his chin sparkled under the fluorescent bathroom lights. His parents must have noticed and notified their housekeeper to add a shaver to the weekly shopping list. It had shown up on his bathroom counter one day, unexpectedly.

His wavy hair was a lighter brown than Leana's, and always well-groomed. During the summer it turned auburn, and his skin easily tanned. This accentuated his deep blue eyes, especially if he wore any shade of blue. His father had frowned at Jonathon the last time they visited the barber shop when his son requested they NOT cut much off his hair length. It was unlike him to question his father and his request earned him a long hard stare and a raised eyebrow before Mr. Samuels reluctantly agreed with a slight nod, peering momentarily at Jonathon over his glasses before returning to read his *New York Times* newspaper.

If Jonathon had any advantage over JR, it was less acne, perhaps from the lack of greasy fast food. While growing up, Jonathon's family seldom ate out. And until their conflicting schedules began to get in the way of daily rituals, the Samuels' little family of three often enjoyed their meals with place settings of fine china and silver and were always home-cooked and earnestly prepared by their beloved help, Lulu. She was a Filipino woman who claimed to have gone to culinary school before coming to the States. Her English was polished, having been held to the high standards in the Samuels household for the past 18 years. Although, her speech often became indecipherable if someone got her angry, causing her to speak at the speed of light. And when she was being silly or playful, she ignored grammatical verbiage.

Lulu frequently and lovingly told others her Jon-Jon "has the cutest dimples when he smiles." After all, she practically raised him until the time he was old enough to put on a suit and sit still long enough to accompany his parents without being disruptive. She had been a nanny and playmate, a chef, a seamstress and even a tutor during his elementary days. Her great insight helped him with creating school projects that required patience his parents sometimes lacked. She had taken a step back in recent years as his mother and father's influences grew more prominent in his life. But she was always available to give him advice if he was being bullied at school or got angry with his parents, as boys do.

Lulu was quite young when she first began working for their family. Although she never married nor been a parent, it was now her, not his mother or father, who noticed her Jon-Jon beginning to act differently. Since his parents were preoccupied with their own relationship problems lately, Lulu decided one morning to take it upon herself to adopt a motherly role and pry a little.

She peered into Jonathon's room through a barely cracked bedroom door, finding him sitting hunched over his computer looking forlorn.

"Jon-Jon? What is on your mind these days, boy?" she asked in her usual straightforward way. Wearing a sly grin, she pushed her way through the door to deliver a stack of clean and neatly pressed shirts to his closet drawers. "You look like you've lost your puppy... only I know you ain't got no puppy!" (She also ignored her grammar when teasing or to lighten his mood.)

She stood at barely 5' tall, with a cherry patterned apron wrapped around her rotund hips. Scurrying about the room tidying up, she did not break her stride as she waited for Jonathon to answer. If she had to, she could make her way around the entire house with her eyes closed, but as instructed, she always stayed away from Jonathon's desk except for a light dusting. Even at three years old, Jonathon made it clear, throwing near tantrums, that he did not like his projects touched by anyone. His parents thought this was cute. Lulu thought it was his way of keeping control over something in his life.

Jonathon started tinkering with electronics at an early age, beginning when his Aunt Frances from California sent him an elaborate science kit for his fourth birthday, complete with Bunsen burners and walkie-talkies. Lulu immediately hid the Bunsen burner, saving it until he was a bit older. But his obvious knack with gadgets manifested in those preschool years as he would often sit with utter fascination in front of any science television show that explained how things worked. He made something out of any scrap of anything in the house or garage.

This preoccupation frequently benefitted the Samuels at long drawn-out events where most kids would have been bored to oblivion. Instead, Jonathon would kindly ask for coins, string, wrappers, paperclips, etc. from the pockets and purses of other guests. Then he would happily proceed to conjuring up strangely, beautiful, and even occasionally, useful gadgets or artwork.

Unable to ignore her question, Jonathon slowly lifted his head toward Lulu. "You know me *too* well, Lulu," wondering with each syllable if this was possible.

She took this as an offer to briefly interrupt her official household duties. Shutting the door gently behind her, she walked over and sat on the end of the bed. Jonathon resumed his head-down position and began massaging his temples as if in pain, hoping she wouldn't stay long.

"What's her name?" Lulu asked, quite confidant she had hit the nail on the head.

Jonathon leaned back in the chair and arched his neck backwards over the seatback so that he was now viewing Lulu from upside down.

"I wasn't born yesterday, you know!" she retorted to his look.

Jonathon swung his chair around suddenly to face Lulu directly. He took a deep sigh and held his breath in anticipation of what was about to come out of his mouth. "Aaaaaaah!" he let out a sorrowful moan before recoiling and dropping his head to his hands once again. They both were quiet for a moment. Jonathon was searching for words. Lulu was considering running out the door. Finally, she heard him whisper a barely audible "Leana."

Lulu nodded, proud to have reached the correct assumption. "Hmm, I see." Seldom speechless, she paused to compose herself a moment as she realized with a bit of surprise what her Jon-Jon had just admitted. She knew this would be a delicate subject.

"Can I assume from your gloomy mood, that there is a problem with this 'Miss Leana'?"

Jonathon lifted his head again and took off his glasses, rubbing his eyes. Lulu had a panicky feeling for a moment that maybe there was something more wrong than she originally imagined. But Jonathon's next words gave her comfort that this was nothing more than unexplored feelings of a first crush.

"Aww…I don't know, Lulu. I keep thinking about her. She barely knows I exist…but actually, she does because we've worked together in class. She just doesn't know I think about her…" He paused a few seconds as Lulu bit her lip waiting for him to go on. Jonathon gave a quick glance up to notice Lulu's caring expression. Feeling safe, he continued. "Well, what I mean…she doesn't know… in a way, I kind of wish…" He paused again and looked up at the ceiling while searching for the right words. Although his sentences weren't making any sense, Lulu was following him perfectly.

"I don't know how to put it," he puffed each word slowly. "She is just so…so…" He took a deep sigh and let out another rather loud, abrasive moan. "Ughhh! But she has this boyfriend!" He spit out the word 'boyfriend' as if it was poisonous. "She acts all weird around him. I wish she'd act that way around me…even though I don't know what I'd do if she did." He turned to Lulu with the utmost sincerity. "What makes girls act weird around guys? I'd honestly like to know."

Jonathon had barely taken a breath. So, when he finished with a question it caught Lulu off guard. "Um, well, Jon-Jon. Girls can act quite strange for lots of reasons. It's hard to know what she's thinking. Maybe you don't want her to act like that around you. Maybe that means she's comfortable around you and can be herself." Lulu tried offering excuses, but she could tell Jonathon wasn't buying it from the way he screwed up his mouth and rolled his eyes.

She considered what advice she could offer and spoke cautiously. "Maybe she just *thinks* she likes this other guy, but it isn't real because she doesn't really know him?" She shrugged her shoulders and ended the sentence in a questioning way as Jonathon returned a doubtful look. "Is he some big shot guy that acts all tough around her? She may find out he's not all that and change her mind. Maybe if you try talking to her a little, she'll get to know you better and then…who knows?"

Jonathon gave a smug grin and a thumbs-up to Lulu as he once again buried his head in his folded arms atop his desk, letting her know he'd heard enough. She seemed to take it as a thanks. Deep down, he knew she was only trying to boost his confidence, but her pep talk wasn't providing any concrete answers to his problem.

The only thing certain in Jonathon's mind was he couldn't wait to see Leana again. He thought about her up until he went to bed and closed his eyes each night. He set his phone alarm ringtone to a song he heard her humming once at the beginning of the year. He knew the last part of the route she walked to school, and even though one might call it stalking, he found ways to run into her at different places around the school campus throughout the week. He had come to hate the weekends, knowing there was little chance of seeing her during this time. One weekend, recently, he did catch a glimpse of her getting picked up in front of a strip mall by a woman he presumed was her mom. Jonathon had been practicing his behind-the-wheel driving lesson down Bishop Street in the middle of town with his father sitting in the passenger seat keeping a watchful eye on his son's abilities. Fearing his dad would criticize his driving if he slowed the car down to take a closer look, Jonathon simply made a mental note of where he spotted Leana in case it was one of her regular pit-stops. Whenever in the area, he would surely be on the lookout.

Knowing Leana had a boyfriend, few things gave Jonathon hope of striking up a relationship with her. But he noticed she did always stop to say hello whenever they crossed paths and even started giggling at their last meeting, saying it was so funny how often they ran into each other. *I'd better be careful to not be obvious,* he thought to himself.

Lulu stood up and patted Jonathon's shoulder. "It will all work out, you'll see, Jon-Jon." Walking toward the door she pointed at his many gizmos and gadgets splayed across his corner desk. "You should just build a machine that will make her like you better," she joked as she left his room.

Jonathon wasn't in a joking mood, but he closed his eyes rehashing Lulu's words of advice as he heard her footsteps transcending the hardwood stairs to the kitchen. He began swaying side to side in his swivel chair and took a couple of long, deep breaths. Swinging to the left until it would twirl no further...then swinging to the right and back again.

Jonathon started feeling dizzy when suddenly an incredible idea began to form in his spinning brain. He recalled his mom talking on the phone recently with her sister, his Aunt Anna. When she got off the phone, his mom couldn't stop laughing as she sat at the dinner table telling Jonathon and his dad that her sister had a dream about the UPS delivery man who drops off packages regularly. Apparently, the dream seemed so real to Aunt Anna, she now felt giddy and often blushed whenever the man came to the door with another delivery. As Jonathon's mom told the story, their small family couldn't stop laughing, joking that Aunt Anna's dreams meant she had been divorced too long.

Jonathon pressed his heels to the ground to stop the twirling chair and bolted upright. *Maybe a little complicated, but brilliant,* he thought. Hardly able to contain himself, he opened the lid to his laptop and wasted no time getting down to business. Frantically typing the ideas now pouring into his head, he knew the amount of research it would take to formulate and design his newfound project. Still, he felt sure he had the intelligence and creativity to make it happen. *Why haven't I thought of this before*? he thought with anxious excitement. But actually, Jonathon hadn't come up with the idea. Lulu had.

(4 months later)

Jonathon's parents reluctantly kept him in public school after their gifted son literally fell into a mini depression at the mere mention of changing him to a private school when he was in third grade. Their suburban neighborhood, manicured with draping trees along pristine sidewalks and chiseled landscaping, was one of the safest in the state. The town of Eagleview was largely middle class, having highly regarded schools and teachers. So, when their little Jonathon pleaded to remain with all his childhood friends, Mr. and Mrs. Samuels discussed the matter and decided to give it a try. They made him promise to never let his grades falter if he wished to remain in his current school. Jonathon was so overjoyed, he even scrawled out a promissory note in his handwriting, complete with a date and signature and hand-delivered it to his parents that evening at the dinner table.

Now in high school, Jonathon walked down the hall at Cascadia High feeling the familiar sense of urgency always present prior to the first class of the day. Slamming of locker doors and hurried chatter and footsteps could be heard in every direction. He took a deep breath, taking in the smell of freshly prepared cafeteria food wafting from the kitchen. By the end of fourth period when the kitchen closed, that smell would be replaced with the mustiness of the familiar two-story plastered walls.

He weaved in and out of the myriad of students, many of whom he at least recognized from one class or another in past years. He couldn't help but wonder how many of them were daydreaming of being somewhere else. *Were they having a bad day but still forcing a fake smile? Which ones are suffering sleepless nights because of problems at home, or with their boyfriend or girlfriend? Who is acting the role of popular and confident but deep inside feeling insecure and scared?* Unable to read the minds behind the many faces, he couldn't help but wonder what they were thinking. The hours and hours of research and time put into his project over the last four months led him now to an obsession with thinking of how the brain works.

He scanned the corridor looking for his best friend, Jasper, expecting him to be camped out in front of their shared locker. Jasper did not disappoint. Jonathon quickly spotted Jasper's wiry mismanaged afro, which stood out amongst the mostly Caucasian school population. His friend was propped up against the row of metal doors, biting his nails. He was waiting for Jonathon to make his way through the crowds, hoping for his daily update on the progress of Jonathon's project in the five minutes left before class.

He and Jasper had been best friends since the second grade, the year Jasper's family moved to their sleepy little town. It was the first time Jonathon had a black kid in his class and he found it curiously compelling to befriend the new boy. When Jonathon introduced himself and said he wanted to be his first friend at his new school, Jasper quickly put him in his place by informing Jonathon that he had plenty of friends already, then gibed he would be happy to add him to the list. This made the young, naïve Jonathon very happy at the time, as he didn't yet understand sarcasm. He was just happy to romp around with this new, lively and spunky personality. Jonathon envied Jasper's quick wit and humor and how he could always hold a conversation, unlike some playmates who preferred physical activities on the playground over sitting quietly to learn strategic board games. Likewise, Jasper envied Jonathon's nerdy and brilliant mind and felt challenged by Jonathon's intellect. Within a few short weeks, the two began meeting in corners of the schoolyard to play card games during recess and lunch, and eventually they began hanging out at Jonathon's house after school to build elaborate science projects and other gizmos. Lulu often teased them about being inseparable, however, their close friendship created a bond envied by their classmates.

"So, Jon my buddy...any progress?" Jasper lifted his eyebrows awaiting his friend's update. He was hanging on the locker door while Jonathon scrounged through the shelf looking for his English notebook. Being the same height, they were eye to eye.

"Ya. I think it's almost ready. I was up half of the night last night trying to tweak the last little glitches. I almost tried it out..." he paused as Leana walked by with a small group of girlfriends giggling and whispering to each other. He lost concentration of what he was saying to Jasper.

"O...K...?...and...?" Jasper prodded, rolling his eyes when he realized the source of Jonathon's distraction.

"Well, I THINK I'm about ready. I want you to try it. I mean... just come over and we can test it out on you."

"Hey! We talked about this. I'm not your guinea pig. It kind of creeps me out a little. I mean...messing with someone's brain? It seems wrong!" Jasper took a step away and started pacing and flaring his hands around in Jasper fashion. "I kind of like the way I am." He puffed out his chest and bobbed his head as he strutted back and forth in front of the locker nervously. His coiled, wiry hair pulsated above his head as he paced, reminding Jonathon of a rooster with attitude. Jonathon chuckled to himself but remained stoic to let Jasper know he was serious.

The two locked eyes, holding a stare before Jasper continued. "What if it does something crazy like electroshock therapy or something freaky? Why don't you go ahead and try it out on YOU first if you were thinking about doing it anyway?" He sarcastically threw in the last question without expecting an answer.

Jonathon continued to glare at his friend, long enough to come up with a rebuttal. "If I input a dream, I might dream about it just because I came up with it!" He kept his voice low but stern. "You said you trusted me. All we have to do is attach a couple of wires to your scalp with little sticky pads for about ten minutes and then you listen to some music through headphones. It's not going to SHOCK you! If it works, it'll just give you a really cool dream. Whatever dream you want! Come on, Jaz..." Jonathon scanned his mind to come up with something Jasper might like to dream about. "What if...I give you a dream about being out on the lake all day and catching more fish than you ever imagined! Huge ones!"

Jasper grabbed ahold of the locker again and looked away, contemplating his options. He side-eyed Jonathon with a skeptical frown as Jonathon stood gripping his books, still not releasing his stare-down.

"Come on! You can do better than that!" Jasper then eyed a cute, blonde cheerleader walking by and winked at Jon. "I wouldn't mind dreaming about *her*." He flicked his eyebrows up and down as he watched the girl prance by. When he looked back at Jonathon and sensed his growing impatience, Jasper sighed, throwing his arms out. "Okay, okay! I'll think about it overnight. Give me one more night to embrace having a half-normal brain," he quipped while rolling his eyes, then kicked the locker door shut.

Jonathon smiled and slapped his friend on the back and gave his shoulder a squeeze. "You won't be sorry, buddy! In fact, you are so going to thank me."

"I didn't say yes. I said I would *think* about it." Jasper quickly clarified his intent.

"Ya...well, close enough." Jonathon laughed, still patting his back as the two of them turned to zigzag through the few students left scurrying to class before the bell. Entering the first period English class they shared, the two slithered into the only available seats, which happened to be in the front row. Leana was not in their first period class, and Jonathon felt it refreshing to start his day not distracted by her presence. Although, excitement over his invention and its prospective benefits made it difficult for him to concentrate on *anything* else these past few months.

The night Lulu first planted the seed that sparked the idea of a Dream Machine, Jonathon wasted no time getting down to business. He initially did research on dreams...everything from ancient alchemy, Sigmund Freud's lifelong studies, receptivity in lucid dreams and sleep cycles. He grazed the Internet filled with a wealth of information on similar related research, both old and new.

He learned that through computerized brain imaging and science available, researchers found that the brain becomes de-activated when people dream. Jonathon found it fascinating to discover the section of the brain partly responsible for one's own volition and decisions kind of… shuts down during dreams. And when that happens, another part of the brain, the limbic region that controls emotions, kicks in. Those emotions find their way into dreams by bringing up similar memories of that particular emotion from the past.

As he read on, he also learned about how the brain goes into a stage called REM (rapid eye movement) during dreaming and that a lot of studies have been aimed at helping people to try to control their dreams. Jonathon's mind and skills in technology went to work around the clock. Lulu would often tap on his door and peek in to say hello with her suspicious eyes and ask what in the world was keeping him up so late. He would fib and say he was dutifully studying for another test. Now, as he sat watching his English teacher Mr. Bramble scribble vocabulary words across the white board, he felt his lack of sleep attacking his heavy eyelids. He spent so much time on his new machine but hadn't really formulated a plan yet on how he was going to execute the next step. His goal was to come up with an excuse to invite Leana to his house and get her use the machine. He would program a dream about himself and if all went as he hoped, she would be dreaming and having adoring thoughts about Jonathon that very night. These circulating thoughts would eventually persuade her subconscious that her feelings from the dream were real. *A great plan*, Jonathon thought, but he wasn't exactly sure what kind of dream he should create for her or how he was going to get her over to his house. Sitting in class contemplating the possibilities, Jonathon was snapped out of his fog abruptly when Mr. Bramble cleared his throat loudly. His teacher was staring directly at him.

"I can assume you know the answer, Mr. Samuels?" he asked as he sauntered toward Jonathon's desk. Several of the kids in class murmured and snickered.

"Um, can you please repeat the question, Mr. Bramble?" Jonathon asked straightening up, trying to disguise his inattentiveness.

Classroom chuckles grew as Mr. Bramble, who did sincerely like his brilliant student, stooped to come face to face with Jonathon and grinned ear to ear like a Cheshire cat. Jonathon's face turned from notepaper white to the red of a barely ripened strawberry. He stretched his back to arch slightly away from his teacher's grinning face.

"No real question, Mr. Samuels. It just isn't like you to be sleeping on the job in my class. Please sit up straight and pay attention while I go over the upcoming test." Mr. Brambles' embarrassment of Jonathon was enough to keep him alert for the rest of the period as he and Jasper frequently exchanged glances.

When the bell rang, Jasper met him just outside in the corridor. "Smooth move," Jasper poked at Jonathon.

"Yah, well, I'm operating on very little sleep. I'm heading to study hall for a snooze. I'll catch you later?" Jonathon hoisted his backpack over his shoulder.

"Later," Jasper offered back with a knuckle bump to his friend's upper arm.

Jonathon wove through the hall, vaguely aware of his surroundings. His late nights really were catching up with him. What he needed was a few good, long-night's sleep to catch up. When he entered the courtyard area that supplied study tables and computers for students between classes, he made his way over to one of the only vacant tables nestled in the corner and unloaded his backpack and cellphone.

He swung the cafeteria-style chair around, straddled it backwards and leaned against the wall, stretching out his long legs. He set the alarm on his cell phone for 25 minutes just in case he happened to lapse into more of a coma than a light sleep. Tucking his phone into his jacket pocket, he slumped back and closed his eyes and began thinking again about the possibilities of dreams for Leana.

Near sheer exhaustion, Jonathon felt glad the weekend was coming up. His mind drifted as he relaxed, then with very little effort, he devised a simple plan. Tonight, he'd try out his machine by programming a dream for himself. Scrolling his thoughts for what that dream might be, Jonathon's body began to surrender to fatigue.

Exactly 25 minutes later, he lurched when his phone alarm rang one of his favorite cartoon tunes. He dug it out of his pocket to quickly turn it off before the noise disturbed other students. While scanning the room, he noticed Leana seated directly across the large study area talking to her baseball hunk, JR. Mindlessly watching them, a mischievous grin crossed his face as he imagined the possibilities. *Tonight*, he thought, *Leana will be mine in my dreams.* His trance was broken, and his smile faded to a panicked somber look when he realized Leana was staring straight back at him with a puzzled look on her face.

"Oh my God," he murmured, wondering if he might have said her name out loud inadvertently. He tried to act busy, leaning over his backpack which was on the ground at his feet, rummaging through it for nothing in particular. Wondering how obvious his thoughts were to Leana or others, he felt small beads of sweat forming across his forehead while trying to remain calm, sensing she was still watching him. His heart was pounding.

While shoving his books back into place inside the backpack, he could hear footsteps coming toward him. *Please, dear God*, he thought. *Let it be someone else.* He turned his head slightly and caught sight of a pair of black Ugg boots pointing straight at him.

"Jonathon?" He jerked his head up quickly, smacking it on the side of the study hall table.

Loud snickers emanated across the room. Embarrassed, he fought back the urge to rub the now throbbing area on his head.

Looking up into Leana's brown eyes, his stomach knotted up and he felt like a weighted blanket had just fallen on him.

"Hey, Leana. How's it going?" he greeted her nonchalantly and wiped his brow with his jacket sleeve, not only to blot the beads of sweat away but also to hide his eyes that were now watering from the sting of his injury.

"Are you…okay? You looked really spacey. I was worried you were on drugs or something," she asked with concern. When Jonathon looked back down, she grimaced and cleared her throat. "Just kidding. I know you wouldn't…you know…use drugs. But, seriously, are you…okay?"

Bursting out a loud chuckle to mask his humiliation, Jonathon quickly came up with an excuse. "Um...I was just thinking about something funny that happened last week with Jasper and was kind of zoning, I guess." Before she had a chance to respond or break away to go back to her group, Jonathon jumped at a chance to engage her in small talk. "How are you? Making any headway on that chemistry project?" he asked, trying to divert the topic of conversation away from himself.

"No, not yet. I'm glad it's not due for a while. Chemistry isn't my forte. I'll probably put it off as long as possible." Her dimples complimented the waves in her cascading hair, making it difficult for Jonathon to not gawk. A brief silence fell between them. "Um, well, I just wanted to make sure you were okay. I'll see you in class." She gave a quick little wave of her hand as she turned to leave.

"Okay. See ya. Thanks for the concern!" he called out with a little laugh as he watched her sashay back toward her group of friends. When he noticed JR in the distance glaring at him, Jonathon abruptly did a nosedive toward the backpack sitting at his feet.

Quickly, he gathered his belongings and zigzagged between the crowded tables filled with serious studiers and casual gossipers alike. He felt he couldn't escape the room fast enough. The next class was chemistry, but he wouldn't be trying to sit near Leana as he usually did. Too awkward, he felt. Soon, they would be working together on their final lab project and he hoped to spend plenty of time with her then.

Rounding the corner toward class, Jasper was in the hall talking to their longtime friend, Kate Wyatt.

Kate and Jonathon had gone to the same elementary school since day one, so she also knew Jasper well. Living close to both boys, they all became good friends from years of walking similar routes to and from school. Kate was pretty, in a simple way. She had straight, sandy-colored, shoulder length hair and hadn't yet begun wearing makeup like most other girls in their grade, but in Jonathon's opinion, she wouldn't be as pretty if she did. He didn't see her in the same way he did Leana—Kate was just one of his buddies, though he did find it difficult to not notice recent changes in her developing body.

Jasper didn't look at Kate *that* way either, as far as Jonathon knew. To each of them, she was simply a friend who happened to be a girl.

"Hey Jasp...Kate." Jonathon greeted them both as he approached.

"What's up?" Jasper asked. "Your face looks all flushed like you've been working out." "Long story," mumbled Jonathon under his breath. He brushed past them. "Later." He continued down the hall without giving either of his friends an explanation, leaving Kate looking exasperated.

"Nice talking to ya!" Kate called out sarcastically, but Jonathon ignored her and continued walking without turning around. She looked at Jasper. "He seems preoccupied." She scowled and then glanced back down the hall.

"You have *NO* idea, Kate." Jasper raised his eyebrows as he watched his best friend disappear into the crowd. "I gotta get going. See ya." He, too, rushed off without looking back, wanting to avoid Kate pressuring him with questions.

Standing paralyzed for a moment, Kate's mind was spinning. But as much as she wondered, she could never imagine what was really going on.

Sitting perched on a step stool inside his vast closet, Jonathon sat with wires stringing from the newly built Dream Machine to two small electrodes stuck on each side of his head. His machine had been hidden in the corner, covered by a stack of neatly folded sweaters and a few strategically placed jackets, in case Lulu came in. He had rushed home from school after making excuses to Jasper and Kate, so he wouldn't have to dawdle with them on the walk home. Today, Jasper hadn't even tried to stop him, and Jonathon knew why. He was very aware his friend was not keen on coming over to try out his invention and, therefore, keeping a safe distance.

He buckled down to work on homework, so he could complete it all before going downstairs for dinner. Later, after practically inhaling his meal, he avoided lying to his parents by saying he needed to head upstairs for the night to finish a project. *True enough*, he thought. Secluding himself in his room, he carried his Machine over near the closet and set the aluminum, toaster-sized box onto the carpeted floor, then plopped down to sit crossed-legged next to it.

First, he scribbled a few notes about what he wanted to dream onto a pad of paper—ideas he'd been thinking about all day. While contemplating his options, he began doodling a sketch of his Machine. Jonathon loved drawing and got lost in thought. Soon, he found himself drawing details and labeling knobs and wires he then linked to the head of a stick person wearing headphones. He chuckled at what looked like a pre-school cartoon, then folded the sketch into a paper airplane and flung it across the room. It landed on the back side of his desk, making him laugh out loud.

Deciding it was time, he opened a pack of electrodes. Peeling the backing from one small square adhesive, he placed it on his left temple, attaching the wire he'd marked "left." Then he repeated with one to his right side. Gently sliding the studio quality headphones over his ears, he picked up the microphone and eased back against a small bean bag cushion to relax.

He peeked at his notes one last time before closing his eyes. Then, speaking into a small microphone, he commanded the scenario he hoped to dream. Nervous about his first attempt, he found himself sympathizing with Jasper's hesitancy but shook his head quickly to clear that thought. The dream he input was simple, one in which Leana looked as she did that very day in study hall. But in the dream he programmed, she would come to sit beside him and flash flirtatious smiles as she offered to share her plate of French fries. The two of them would gradually scoot closer and closer together as they talked intimately, getting better acquainted.

Perspiration beads began to form on his forehead. He stopped dictation and took a deep, long breath. He felt afraid to take it any further and simply decided to end with her kissing him on the cheek as they made their way back to class. Setting the microphone down, a warm flush trickled over his face. He found a clean, lone sock lying at the top of a stack of folded clothes and grabbed it to dab the sweat now dripping toward his eyes. Sitting for a moment, he fanned his face with an empty binder trying to temper his emotions. He wondered if he spent too much of his childhood with Lulu watching classic love stories on TV for him to come up with something he had not yet experienced first-hand. Ultimately, not wanting to change a thing, he finalized his recording input by typing in vivid details of each action. Taking a deep breath, he paused only slightly before hitting the save button.

Next, he needed to add music to go with the dream. Browsing through his playlist, he found no songs reminding him of Leana. However, one new song he'd recently downloaded sounded fitting. It was titled "Waiting on a Dream." Jonathon listened to the song to make sure the words weren't completely corny or about something irrelevant. Then keeping the headphones on, he opened an app for dubbing music and overlapped the folky ballad to softly play in the background during the programmed dream. He hit the ON button and rested his head back in his locked hands. The song he chose was melodic and he could feel his shoulders relaxing as it played. He hoped his brain was absorbing the subliminal, detailed messaging through the electrodes. His mind began to wander and before long he dozed off. When Jonathon awoke abruptly thirty minutes later, he bolted up and began peeling the electrodes off his temples as he stood, stretching his neck muscles by tilting his head from side to side. Then he picked up his Machine to set it and the electrodes down on his desk next to his phone. As he did, he noticed a text from Lulu:

U **want dessert?**

Thank goodness Lulu liked today's technology and used texting to avoid making unnecessary trips upstairs. *A knock on the door would have disrupted his programming on the machine,* he thought.

Thanks Lulu. I'm good, he replied. Then he typed a quick **Catch ya tomorrow** to Jasper, so he'd know he was over and out for the night. No reply came back, which probably meant Jasper had either crashed in front of the TV or less likely over a textbook.

Jonathon then crawled under his celestial-printed bed covers. Reaching over to turn off the bedside lamp, he laid back with a smile and a prayer that his dream machine would work. It was barely past 9:00 p.m., much earlier than he usually went to bed. But his eyelids felt heavy, and he knew that even if his Machine didn't work, he definitely needed sleep.

Jonathon woke around 3:00 a.m. with a smile on his face and found himself uttering Leana's name. It all seems so real, he thought. He kept his eyes closed and tried hard to fall back into the dream, but excitement about his Machine working clashed against his efforts to fall back asleep.

It seemed like only moments later when his alarm sounded, and he shot up out of bed. Again, he had been right in the middle of a conversation with Leana during another dream and he thought his alarm was the school bell. Giddiness helped him wake up as he realized he had two similar dreams in one night! In both dreams he was having fun, flirtatious moments with Leana. Elated, Jonathon jumped up and danced around the room barely remembering what day of the week it was. His head was spinning with the possibilities of what this success meant. He couldn't wait to tell Jasper. He couldn't wait to try it out again! And...he couldn't wait to eventually try it out on Leana. All he needed to do was program what he wanted her to dream about and...*the possibilities were endless!*

A soft tap on the door took Jonathon by surprise, sobering his elation. He shook his arms and legs with one last shimmy to calm himself and opened his door. His mother was standing, clutching the front of her robe with one hand and holding a cup of coffee with the other.

"Good morning, honey. Everything okay? I just came up from the kitchen. Sounded like a party going on in there."

"Oh sorry, mom." He hesitated. "I was just doing a couple of jumping jacks to wake up." he lied.

She leaned up on her tiptoes to kiss his forehead. "You sure have been staying up late. How are your classes?" She took a sip of her coffee.

"Lots of homework, as usual."

He noticed his mother's weary look, more so than a typical early morning. "How about you, mom? You haven't been down to breakfast lately. And you look really tired."

"Oh, Jonathon." She leaned in for a hug. "I just haven't been sleeping well." She raised her cup. "Don't you worry. Nothing a little caffeine can't cure." Her smile seemed forced as she turned to head toward her bedroom. "Be careful in there," he heard her warn.

"Ya, I might hurt myself with jumping jacks." Jonathon rolled his eyes and chuckled as he closed his door. "Have a good day, mom."

He hopped into the shower. "I am a freakin' genius!" he shouted melodically as the hot water sprayed over his body. When he got out and was getting dressed, he found it difficult to contain his sheer joy. He rushed around, making adjustments in his room to hide his Machine in case Lulu came in to clean. Throwing on a tee shirt and cords, he felt like gliding down the stair bannister as he'd seen actors do in Broadway musicals. Jumping off the fourth step from the bottom of the stairway to the foyer below, he almost twisted his ankle. His father rounded the corner just in time to see Jonathon correcting his near awkward fall. Eyeing his father's peculiar stare, Jonathon cleared his throat as he tried his best to calm down.

"Well, good morning, Jon." His father greeted him, clearly amused. "You're down a bit earlier than usual." Jonathon barely noticed his father's already perfectly dressed ensemble as this was so typical for him nearly every day of the week. "Lulu made some coffee and is just starting breakfast."

"I, uh, fell asleep kind of early last night, so I didn't need to hit my snooze today." He laughed, wishing he could simply blurt out his joyous news to his dad.

"Well, it's nice to see you for a bit before I head off to work." His dad laid his hand on Jonathon's shoulder and gave it a pat before the two turned to walk down the hall to the kitchen.

Family portraits of formal sittings from nearly every special occasion in the family's past lined the walls; some with just Jonathon in his growing years, some with family members and relatives Jonathon barely remembered. He'd been in friends' houses where photos were more casual snapshots in non-matching frames that looked spontaneous and of real life. He only recently began realizing his family's money afforded some of these gentle luxuries, like the formal family portraits framed with elegant linen matting, things that do not necessarily make one's life any more important.

Lulu greeted the two of them with her big happy smile as they entered the kitchen. "Jon-Jon. You're up early, child! Want some cocoa or coffee…or tea?"

"I'd like a half cocoa and half coffee please." Jonathon slumped down into the dining chair.

Lulu turned around with a raised eyebrow and a half smile. "What do I look like, a barista from The Coffee Couch?"

The three of them all chuckled as the two men of the house sat themselves down at the kitchen dining table. "Thank you, Lulu." Jonathon drew out the words in a mocking but loving tone. He picked up the local section of the newspaper as his father collected the business news, a morning ritual Jonathon loved when the two of them had time. Thumbing through, Jonathon skimmed a few articles about the city's newest remodel of their library and city hall. There was to be a grand opening this coming weekend. He also read about two scholar athletes of the week. *Great,* he thought, noticing one of the athletes was none other than Leana's hunk, JR. Jonathon nodded a smug approval, thinking that the grainy news photo was not a flattering picture of him. He read on and discovered information about a school dance he had vaguely been made aware of through small talk in class. He pulled out his phone and entered the event on his phone calendar.

"What's up?" his father asked.

"Oh, just marking when the school dance is, in case I want to go," he remarked nonchalantly.

His father set his portion of the paper down slowly and peered over his glasses in much the same way he had at the barbershop years before. "You haven't mentioned going to any dances in the past. That's great, son. Where is the dance being held? Meadowland Hall downtown? Or Riverfront?" Riverfront was an elite area along the river, which had facilities that frequently hosted many functions such as conventions and wedding receptions.

"No, dad, actually, this isn't THAT nice. It's just a spring dance held in the gym at school." He suddenly felt a little awkward as he explained what he knew. This really WAS unchartered territory for him. All the years of his cotillion classes were intended to prepare Jonathon for more formal occasions. When his father sat with a blank stare, not responding, Jonathon continued, "They're calling it a 'Garden Party' on the flyers…whatever that means."

His father grinned and nodded several times before speaking. "Well, I'm sure it will be nice," his father finally said, surprising

Jonathon. Returning his focus to the newspaper he then asked without looking up, "Do you have a girl in mind…to invite?"

Jonathon flinched and nervously picked up a spoon to stir his coffee drink. "Not really," was all he managed to get out as he tried to look busy with his portion of the paper. He avoided looking up toward Lulu as he imagined her wearing a sly grin, knowing of his secret affection for Leana.

"I hear most kids just go without a date," Lulu added quickly and then offered more creamer for their coffees, trying to change the subject for Jonathon's sake. She knew him too well. Jonathon then mouthed a thank you to Lulu when he knew his father wasn't watching.

The remainder of the breakfast time was more silent than conversive, so Jonathon politely excused himself. He was eager to get to school and share everything with Jasper.

Once he managed to leave the house, he started whistling as he strolled in the direction of the school. He felt euphoric and didn't wipe the grin from his face until he intercepted a few friends a block from school who wanted to shoot the breeze for the remainder of the walk. After a brief exchange, he caught sight of Kate up ahead and freed himself from the group to catch up to her.

"Hey, Katie bear...how's it going?"

Kate bowed backwards as if being attacked. "Whoa...you woke up on the right side of bed today!" She giggled and then leaned forward to give him a slow-motion punch in the arm.

"Haaaa...as a matter of fact, I did."

"Better than yesterday!" She winked and let out a chuckle.

"What do you mean?" He acted surprised, but deep down he knew his behavior was more than strange when they last spoke.

"I don't know...you just weren't yourself. But...whatever. Glad you're back." She grinned, showing the same cute dimples she'd had since they first met in kindergarten.

Once inside the school halls, Jonathon began noticing posters announcing the upcoming school dance. They'd probably been hanging on the walls for a few weeks, but he hadn't paid attention until today. It was only a little over a week away now and he wondered if he needed to purchase a ticket or to just show up the night of the dance. He slowed his pace to study the posters and Kate, who was still beside him, slowed as well.

"You thinking of going to the dance?" Kate asked hesitantly as she noticed Jonathon's focus.

He turned and caught a sly grin on her face with quizzical brows. Of course, this seemed odd to her. Kate usually went to every school function and knew he didn't frequent these types of events. He paused before answering, not sure if he wanted to go.

"Maybe...I just noticed the poster and thought there's a first time for everything."

With this, Kate's brows raised up a little further.

"OooooooKaaay," she slurred as she turned to continue down the hall, still eyeing Jonathon.

As they walked, he leaned toward her and tried to mimic her facial expression.

"What's the big deal? You usually go, don't you? Do I need a ticket. . .and a date?"

"Wow, you're serious! I'm down to go. I was thinking of skipping this one so I could study for my Lit mid-term, but if you're going, I am NOT going to miss this!" She nudged him with her armful of books and giggled. "And no, you don't need a ticket. You can buy one at the door…and bring your student ID, dork!" nudging him again with a smile.

Still pushing for more information, he repeated the question. "And, what about...a date? Does everyone just show up alone?" Jonathon acted like he knew that to be the case when Lulu had mentioned it, but he really had no idea. Right now, he just wanted to find out if Leana usually went to the dances. He hoped so, even though she would likely be with JR if she did.

Before Kate could answer, Kendra Lake, probably the best dressed girl in all of Cascadia and a good friend of Leana, came strutting around the corner. Her impeccably smooth, blonde, shoulder-length hair matched her flawless complexion. A small "beauty mark" mole sat next to her lip gloss-pursed lips. Today she shouted out pink with everything from her shoes to her slightly showing bra strap.

"Oh, hi, Kate." She crinkled her nose and acknowledged Jonathon but didn't say anything to him. He didn't really know her as much as he knew *of* her. "Did you happen to take any good notes in last Friday's statistics class? I left early and can't find anyone that has any to share."

Kate set her bundle of books down on the ground and started thumbing through her notebook. "I should have something." She was mumbling under her breath as she rummaged through a handful of papers.

Kendra reached out a hand to Jonathon who was standing around, awkwardly looking down the hall. “Hi. I’m Kendra.”

Kate glanced up at them both. “I’m sorry. You guys have never met?”

As if to answer Kate’s question, Jonathon reached out a hand to Kendra. “Hi. Jon,” he replied, taking her delicate soft hand for a quick shake before sticking his hands back in his pockets and taking a deep breath.

Kendra cocked her head. “I think we might have met somewhere before.” Jonathon shrugged his shoulders as he didn’t remember if they had. “Sorry, I interrupted. Whatcha guys doing?” Kendra asked, seemingly to make any type of conversation.

“I found them!” Kate stood up with some papers in hand smiling at them both. “I can run to the office really quick to make copies, if you want to wait?”

“Thanks, Kate!” Kendra reacted with enthusiasm as Kate fled down the hall, leaving her books at Jonathon’s feet. He looked down at them, feeling bound to that spot. Kendra stood biting the inside of her lip, looking down the hall. The silence felt awkward for them both.

“Um, we were just talking about the dance.” Jonathon turned and gave a nod with his head toward the poster. “Guess everyone is going to be there, huh?”

"Me and my friends usually go. I guess there's actually going to be a local band instead of a DJ at this one." Kendra gave a smile but then turned to look for Kate's return.

Jonathon felt a twinge of excitement figuring her "friends" meant Leana WOULD be there. "I haven't gone to many." *A white lie,* he thought. He hadn't gone to any. "I think I might check it out."

"Well, maybe I'll see you there." Kendra responded, stepping aside as Kate came barreling back down the hall toward them.

Nice girl, thought Jonathon. Of course, Leana would have nice friends.

Jonathon watched Kate and Kendra exchanging papers and then Kate sashayed back toward him and her pile of books as Kendra left for class. Jonathon politely picked up Kate's books and handed them to her.

"Thank you very much." She marched out the words in a militant-style voice and then chuckled, giving him a friendly wink as she hurried off. "I'll catch ya later," she yelled back over her shoulder.

Jonathon scampered off to his locker and then quickly to class before the bell. No sign of Jasper this morning either meant his friend slept in yet again or was avoiding him because he didn't want to play guinea pig to Jonathon's Machine. Jonathon was feeling antsy to share his dream experience with his best friend but at this point he wished he could stand up in front of the class and tell them all about it. He glanced around at his classmates as he sat down. *They'd all think I am insane if I told them,* he thought. Then he imagined the news getting back to Leana. No matter how excited he was, he knew he needed to be discreet with his information.

As difficult as it was to concentrate, Jonathon made a huge effort to pay attention in case Mr. Bramble called on him today. He snuck in a couple of texts to Jasper as he wondered why he wasn't in class but he got no response. *Perhaps Jasper's phone was dead or maybe he lost it;* Jonathon wondered. Jasper *always* responded to him, he thought.

In between first period and study hall, Jonathon taped a note for Jasper inside their locker:

Don't make plans after school. Good news. If you are avoiding me, don't worry. You don't have to do a thing!

Jonathon waited a few more minutes to see if Jasper showed up. He usually saw him by this time. He sent another text before rushing toward the study hall area. Once there, he found a table in the center of the room where a small group of sophomore girls were just leaving. He unpacked his books as he scanned the large room. There was no sign of Leana today. Deciding not to worry about where everyone else was, he plopped down on the uncomfortable cafeteria chair and began to work on his chemistry paper. Within minutes, he felt like weights were attached to his eyelids, so he stood to stretch a little, scanning the concession menu from across the room for a heavily caffeinated drink.

While sauntering across the hall to place an order, a few other not-so-close friends gave him hellos and knuckle-knocks. Jonathon wasn't particularly popular but was well known and generally liked. A sudden vibration in his pants pocket startled him. He pulled out his phone to read a rather long text from Jasper telling him he had been up most of the night in the bathroom from something he'd eaten the night before and had just got up. His text ended, **See you after school if I'm feeling better.** Jonathon wasn't surprised. Jasper had always had a delicate stomach.

Jonathon returned to his table a few minutes later with a giant café mocha. He was glad to have the missing Jasper issue resolved but disappointed he'd need to wait until after school to talk to him. Jonathon blew into his drink to cool it off and took a sip as he began doodling on the outer corner of his chemistry notes. He started making circles around the paper's edge with his pen while thinking about his invention. He hated referring to it as his "Machine" or his "Dream Machine" when talking with Jasper. *What if someone overheard them talking about it? They might start asking questions.* He decided to give his machine a name. After all, he felt a personal connection with the device he'd worked on so tirelessly.

To prevent curious ears from perking at their mention of a girl, he began scanning his brain for male names. Television personalities came to mind first, then politicians, cartoon characters and distant family members. Mulling over the options for a few minutes, he chuckled when remembering his great-uncle Walter who used to come over on holidays. Before anyone else had finished dinner, "Uncle Wally" would go missing. The family always found him later fast asleep in a lounge chair in his father's study snoring away and mumbling nonsense while dreaming. He provided brief entertainment for family members who poked their heads in the room, snickering as they listened.

Jonathon wrote "Wally" across the bottom of his notepad. He whispered it out loud a few times, trying to imagine if it was a good fit. The memory of his great-uncle did make him smile but he ended up scribbling out the name. He reluctantly opened his textbook to study, figuring a perfect name would come to him at a later time.

The café mocha helped keep Jonathon awake but the day itself seemed to drag on forever. During chemistry class, Leana looked pretty in a white lacy tank top, black sweater and a long black skirt and black boots. She sat in the back corner lab station inconspicuous to everyone else but Jonathon. She had one arm draped over her backpack, which was lying on the table. Her head was resting on her arm through much of the lecture as she took notes. Jonathon, sitting along the back row, was close enough to feel her near even though she wasn't at his same workstation. He hoped he could talk to her during the actual lab. Usually, he didn't have as difficult of a time concentrating in class as he was today. Watching her out the corner of his eye, he fantasized about having dreams involving the two of them, ones he could program in his Machine later. He longed for her to see him differently. That was his plan...though he had no idea how he was going to get her to come over to his house, let alone convince her to get wired up to a device.

Never one to neglect his studies, Jonathon tried to clear his head and focus on the lecture from his teacher, Mr. Bell. The end of the period was usually reserved for break-out group discussions and lab projects. Today was an exception as Mr. Bell gave the class question and answer time about an upcoming quiz. Jonathon felt frustrated at not getting any group time with Leana. He nonchalantly looked over his shoulder in her direction and noticed her head hanging and her long hair blocking her face. She was intently texting away on her phone.

Turning back around, he tried to focus on listening to the rest of the class engaging in discussions but his mind kept drifting elsewhere. Occasionally, something came to mind that he thought would be a good addition to a dream, so he scribbled key words on a remote corner of his notebook. When the bell rang, Leana seemed very eager to bolt from class. Jonathon leaped from his seat, scrambling to keep close behind her as she forged her way out between other students. It was difficult for him to not appear obvious. By the time he got out the door he could barely see the back of her head, now several yards away down the hall, engulfed in crowds of students. Standing deflated for a moment he let out a sigh and did an about face toward his next class.

American Government was one of his favorite classes. His elderly teacher kept things interesting by often conducting mock trials and discussing real-life legal situations. The class participation was spirited and made learning fun on most days. Jonathon also enjoyed having a few friends in the class who were on his debate team. He often felt it would be a great class to have in the afternoon instead, when he and his fellow students generally struggled to stay awake after eating lunch. It was obvious that Mr. Kip (short for Kipinger) loved teaching, although he was a bit opinionated at times. The period flew by and before Jonathon knew it, the bell was ringing.

Heading toward his locker, he saw Kate glide by with her best friend, Mia. Mia was quite a bit taller than most girls at the school, which had made her a success on the volleyball team. Not quite as cute as Kate, it was her hunched, gangly posture that made her seem generally less attractive to Jonathon. Jonathon wondered if her poor posture may be due to her height. She seemed to always be trying to lean down to the shorter girls' level during conversations. Unfortunately, it carried over as she walked, causing her to look uncomfortably insecure.

Kate and Mia had been best friends since fifth grade when Mia first moved to the area. She was frequently at get-togethers with their group of friends but because she lived further from school, she took the bus. Not getting the chance to hang out on campus after school or share the walks home, she wasn't as close to Jonathon and Jasper as Kate. Mia was also quieter than Kate; always polite and she mostly agreed with everything Kate said. Jonathon gave them both a nod as they walked past. Kate gave him a quick grin and then reached up to whisper something in Mia's ear.

He turned the other way to head back down the hall and practically ran into Leana who breezed past him, brushing arms in the overcrowded hallway. Jonathon slowed as he watched her dash by, noticing her red swollen eyes. She caught Jonathon's eyes briefly but quickly lowered them. He felt certain she had been crying. Not knowing if he should run after her to ask her if she was okay, he fought off the impulse, deciding it might embarrass her. Besides, he didn't feel like he knew her well enough to pry.

Uncertain of what he wanted to do for lunch, since Jasper wasn't around, Jonathon headed to his locker to put his backpack away and then went to the food court to buy a smoothie. He then went outdoors to get some fresh air and sat on the edge of a brick planter box to people watch while he slurped down his meal.

Thoughts of Leana rocketed through his brain as he wondered what had caused her to cry. Secretly, he hoped it was relationship trouble with "Mr. Baseball." This thought caused him to teeter between feeling hopeful and feeling guilty for thinking such things. He didn't like seeing her upset but if she was going to cry, it may as well have something to do with JR.

He let the guilty thing go and decided it was probably only wishful thinking anyway.

It felt muggy and warm outside, so Jonathon moved to be under a tree and sat on the ground with his back against the trunk. The sun had already broken through the earlier morning haze. For April, the day was warmer than usual, though a few clouds were moving quickly overhead from a breeze he could barely feel down on the ground. It wasn't long before he started to feel sleepy as he let his mind relax without much deliberate thought.

For a change, he began to daydream about a few other things besides his new Machine, things like colleges he might like to visit in the future. Schools on the east coast seemed to appeal to him, but he wasn't sure he'd like their winter weather. His parents promised him a few road trips next summer to visit a few prestigious schools of their choice. *Maybe he would convince them to take him somewhere warm, like California.* With his grades, he knew his choices would be many. But all of that seemed so far off.

His mind drifted back to Leana. He began imagining her as his girlfriend. *What if they stayed together through his senior year? If they went to different colleges, would they break up? And what about leaving his friends like Jasper and Kate?* Kate was like a comfortable shoe. He let out a chuckle, thinking what she might say knowing he referred to her in that way. But truly, she really was someone he felt was always there, a perfectly molded friend, sometimes even more of a friend than Jasper. A rock. A sounding board. Even a partner in crime on many occasions.

Once in middle school, the two of them plotted an innocent joke in the science lab that turned out causing an experiment to go badly, sending out a foul odor, not only in the class (which was the intent) but also throughout most of the hallways. A planned school assembly had to be postponed because of the vile smell. He and Kate avoided getting into trouble since their teacher thought it was an accident.

Jonathon smiled as he remembered that day. It was not in his character to be mischievous but his and Kate's relationship was so fun-loving they just naturally got caught up in the humor of it all. On their walk home that day, they couldn't stop laughing.

A loud ruckus across the campus lawn disrupted his thoughts and he sat up to witness a couple of students pushing and yelling obscenities at each other on the far corner near the street. It was difficult for Jonathon to make out who they were through the crowd. He squinted, hoping to get a better view. Then, as the arguing began to turn physical, he spotted a few other students trying to break up the fight by grabbing hold of the duo's shirt sleeves and pulling them in opposite directions. Jonathon continued watching the disturbance unfold. He wasn't surprised by the many who just walked around the incident as if nothing was happening, barely looking up from their cellphones. Finally, he witnessed another student approaching the scene who seemed to have some clout and size, finally stepping in to break it up.

Jonathon removed his glasses and cleaned off the lenses with the bottom of his shirt. When he put them back on, the small crowd of onlookers were dispersing and clapping. He could now see the two participants were a couple of girls he recognized from a fight earlier in the year. Girl fights often attracted mini crowds who rushed to watch the show. Generally, they began with name calling, ending with them tearing at each other's clothes and hair. Jonathon chuckled to himself and shook his head as he recollected the scenes.

He was about to lie back and open a book when he noticed the person who had ended the fight was passing by and heading toward the front entrance of the school. Jonathon cringed as jealousy infiltrated every pore of his body. The noble hero was none other than JR.

He rolled his eyes and laid back down, shaking off the thoughts of his competitor who had disappeared through the school doors. He, again, wondered if Jasper was going to make it over to his house today. Having to wait to reveal his newest revelations to Jasper was killing him.

Watching the clouds float slowly overhead, he tried to recall his scribbled notes about potential dreams and was trying to put them together in his brain. He wondered if the hours and days' worth of his efforts would turn out to be futile. He didn't have long to ponder as a light kick against his leg and a gawky laugh disrupted his thoughts. It was Reno, a friend from his debate team. "Hey" was his only announcement.

"Hi, Ren. How's it going?" Jonathon slurred, reluctant to engage in a full conversation. He just wanted to relax but that hope had quickly dissolved.

"I was wondering if you knew when practice is scheduled for...I missed class Monday and I think it might be today...?"

Jonathon mumbled something undecipherable under his breath as he quickly got up. He pulled out his phone to look at the calendar. "It IS today. At 5:30." He clamored a long, sustained groan as he realized he'd now have to postpone meeting up with Jasper.

"Oh, man, I was afraid it was today." Reno looked panic-stricken. "Okay. Well, I'll be there. I gotta go take care of something. Catch ya later." Reno gave a thumbs-up as he ran off and Jonathon reciprocated the gesture. Then he leaned back against the tree, massaging his forehead with one hand.

"Dang it!" He loudly muttered to himself. Hesitantly, he typed out a text to Jasper, knowing his friend would be delighted to cancel.

His friends on debate team were as diverse as friends could get. Sarah Jonday was a tall skinny girl with a demure attitude. Her eyebrows were dark and thick, which took away the allure of her green eyes. It was hard not to notice the brows first. Her coal black hair had a blunt cut, almost vogue-looking. She lacked confidence and her eyes were almost always looking down or away even when she was talking directly with someone. However, her shy appearance disappeared once she started debating any topic she felt passionate about. This made her a valuable member of the team.

Bryan Corwin was an athlete on the baseball team along with Leana's JR. Jonathon got the impression from some of their conversations that Bryan sat on the bench most of the time. Jonathon had never attended one of the school's games, so he didn't really know.

Bryan had the mind of a computer, with a head that seemed too small to fit all his knowledge. It looked even smaller when he wore his baseball cap and squished down his short-cut afro. His nose, in contrast, was twice as big as most and was slightly crooked from a direct hit with a baseball in his earlier years. Jonathon really enjoyed his interactions with Bryan even though they had never socialized outside of debate practices and meets.

Jason Bon, a normal enough guy, was the one Jonathon found it the most difficult to bond with in the group. He seldom stuck around to mingle with the rest of the team after events and always acted very businesslike. There were rumors that he and his best friend Nate were "more than friends." Nobody seemed to care these days but Jonathon sensed Jason's evasiveness fueled speculation from others. Jonathon loved having him on the team. He had a memory for details and statistics unmatched by any other teammate from their school.

The only one on the debate team that irritated Jonathan was a girl named Susan Shooflee. She was as short as Sarah was tall. She, too, had black hair only it looked like she'd stuck her finger in a light socket. It sprang in all directions with wiry, non-committed spirals down to the middle of her back. She wore glasses with frames that matched her jet-black hair and because of her height (or lack of) she often had her head cocked back in order to view the world through the bottom portion of her bifocals. She transmitted a snobby air about her and a defensive balk with nearly every confrontation. One afternoon while shooting the breeze, Jonathon and Bryan Corwin decided her attitude likely began in childhood when she had to frequently fend off teasing about her last name. Jonathon tried to be nice to her but was constantly met with her exasperated sighs at even a minute suggestion for the team. He learned that avoiding her was best. Not that her attitude didn't come in quite handy during debates, he just simply couldn't stomach the negativity she emitted on down time. He never sat near her during team meetings.

And then there was Reno Johnson. Gawky in every sense of the word but nice as could be. A walking encyclopedia. His wardrobe consisted of little else than an array of buttoned polo shirts in every dull color on the spectrum. He wore his sandy blonde hair slicked back like a traveling door-to-door salesman.

Every member contributed immensely to their team, which was one of the best in the state. All were exceptionally articulate and well informed about current events. Jonathon's dad had been instrumental in persuading his son to take up debate, and participation on the team was one of the main reasons Jonathon opened the newspaper each morning, unlike most others his age. Jonathan understood the stigma of being nerdy, however, when an announcement was made during a school assembly and their championship team was introduced, a mini frenzy occurred. Now it almost seemed cool to be a member. Fellow students he didn't know would walk by giving a shout-out or wanting to give him a high five with wishes of good luck for the next tournament, even though the season was technically over.

Jonathon pulled himself up from the grass, brushed off his khakis and then lugged his books under his arm to the next class. The rest of the afternoon couldn't go by fast enough.

After school, Jonathan made a quick run home to grab a bite and work on a bit of homework before rushing back out to his 5:30 meeting. He decided to skip the shortcut across the park, his usual route. Instead, he walked a bit further, circling around the park, so he could catch a glimpse of Jasper's house just in case his friend happened to be outside. The two-story brick house looked quiet with all but one of the upstairs' curtains drawn. The sun had set, so it was now dark enough for the warm, yellow glow of a light from the kitchen window to filter through the wood slats of a closed shutter. He figured the family was home but decided he didn't have the time to be led inside by Jasper's gracious parents if he knocked on the door, so he just trudged on toward the school. A couple houses down from Jasper's place, a few grade-school boys were throwing a football around in the front yard. When one sailed past Jonathon's head on a missed catch, they all apologized, laughing as they took off running in the direction of the park to continue playing.

Jonathon looked around, admiring the quaint houses lining the street. As he walked, he began to wonder where Leana lived. He had seen her leaving school, usually in the opposite direction of his own house, and occasionally being picked up by someone in a metallic red SUV. He rounded the corner by the school's entrance and his heart jumped when he noticed an SUV parked in the front-loading zone. It was now too dark outside to tell the exact color, but it looked like the one he had seen Leana get out of in the past.

He picked up his pace until he reached the vehicle, hoping to be lucky enough to have this be her family's car. He slowed his pace when he passed by, trying to inconspicuously side eye the passenger seat. It was difficult to see anything through the tinted windows, but the car appeared empty. *What would she be doing here this late,* he thought? As he turned to go toward the main entrance, he scanned the parking lot to see if she was perhaps hanging out with JR somewhere. The lot seemed quiet, so he decided to go on inside. As he pushed through the door with his hip, he collided with a woman who was trying to exit.

"Oh, excuse me, sorry, ma'am," Jonathon stuttered.

The pretty woman holding a stack of books dismissed him politely and stepped off the curb to walk around to the driver's side of the SUV when one of the books from the pile slipped and fell to the pavement. Jonathan rushed over to pick it up for her.

"Thank you," she said apologetically. Jonathon glanced at her briefly, searching for similarities to Leana's features. Her dark brown hair gave him hope.

"No problem," he replied as he stooped to retrieve the book from the road. As he stood up, he purposefully let the front cover open slightly. There in bold print was Leana's name printed neatly in the top corner.

"Oh, are you Leana's mom?" Jonathon quickly dug deep to get the nerve to ask, even though he already knew.

The woman looked surprised by his question at first, but Jonathon pointed at Leana's name as he handed the book to her, and she gave him a nod. "Yes, I am. I just stopped by for a few of her books and assignments since she might be gone for the remainder of the week."

Jonathan started to stick his hand out to introduce himself but then realized she didn't have a free hand. "Well, I am Jon. I know Leana from chemistry class. Hope she's okay."

"Thank you, Jon...yes, she's fine. Her grandfather...my father-in-law has passed and she's just going to be home with family this week...and for the funeral. Thank you for your concern. I'll let Leana know I ran into you."

"Of course," Jonathon muttered as Leana's mom got into her car. "Tell her if she needs any notes or anything, I'd be happy to lend them to her." He rushed the words quickly before the car door closed, then took a step back and gave a little wave. Even through the darkened glass, there was no denying her resemblance to Leana when she smiled and waved a little thank you back at Jonathon as she drove off.

He turned to rush inside for debate practice now knowing why Leana had been crying. He felt sad for her and wished he could somehow comfort her. When he entered the meeting, his thoughts of sending flowers to Leana, or searching for her house, quickly took a back burner. Susan Shooflee had her back to Jonathon who just entered. She sat ranting to Jason about why they shouldn't...something, something, something...offering their rebuttal before anyone else...something, something. As Jonathon passed by them to join some of the others seated at an adjoining table, he shook his head and rolled his eyes at Jason who was trying not to laugh at Jonathon's reaction. Diving head-on into the meeting helped Jonathon keep his mind off Leana until a quarter after eight when they convened.

On his way home, Jonathon took an extra-long route, zigzagging the closest streets with hopes of spotting the Parkers' red SUV parked in a driveway. He had no luck but still felt determined to find out where Leana lived. Once he got home, he threw himself in front of his computer, but before searching the internet, he realized an easier way. Digging through his desk drawer, he pulled out a packet of orientation papers from the beginning of the year, still unopened. Ripping off the cellophane, he found the school directory and had no problem locating Leana's name, address and home phone number. Not sure what he planned to do with this newfound information, he took a moment to stare at the page before tucking the booklet back into the drawer. Then he leaned back, stretched out his arms and decided to work on another dream.

This time he came up with a one about an encounter with Leana; dropping by her house to console her over her loss. Jonathan figured a dream might give him the confidence he needed to follow through with the idea. He found it difficult to stay awake when his eyelids grew heavier and heavier, but he lasted just long enough to compute the data and connect himself to his Machine before passing out. The following morning, he woke up grinning when he realized the Machine had worked again.

As Jonathon arrived at school that day, he decided to wait for Jasper by their locker, knowing Jasper would probably try to avoid him. Jonathon understood his reasons but felt his best friend just didn't understand that the Dream Machine was harmless. *Simply transmitting a little dream into someone's head couldn't be all that bad,* he thought.

While hanging out waiting by the locker, a friend of his from grade school walked by with the busy crowd of late arriving students who were rushing to their first period classes. He and Jonathon had barely acknowledged each other since the end of grade school when Sol started hanging with a "different" crowd, one that now frequently hung out on the corner down by I-Scream Ice Cream shop, smoking cigarettes and clanging their skateboards on the sidewalk as they jumped the curb to music from someone's boom-box. Jonathon had seen Sol's gang in town and noticed most of the group, like Sol, had long dyed-black hair, except for one very short dude who appeared taller by sporting a Mohawk. A few of the guys had multiple piercings and tattoos, something unfathomable in the Samuel household. Other than appearances, as far as Jonathon knew, Sol and the others were alright guys. He'd never heard any stories of trouble with any of them. Several years had gone by since Jonathon stopped wondering why Sol gradually stopped coming over to his house. Now a little older, he understood it may have been the vast differences in their two families. Sol lived alone with his dad. Mention of his mom never came up past their first meeting in second grade when Jonathon asked Sol when his mom was going to be home and Sol had replied, "Probably never."

Jonathon looked around and spotted the back of Kate's head down the hall by her friend Tessa's locker, deep in conversation with a few girls. He shifted his search in the opposite direction, still watching through the crowd for Jasper.

Suddenly, he felt a thump on his head from a notebook and immediately knew it was Jasper. "Thanks for that." Jonathon turned and tried to flick his hand across Jasper's ducking body.

"You're welcome, Big Dreamer," Jasper coughed out a chuckle.

"Well, you can laugh your way all the way down to my house after school, dude. It works…HAS worked twice and you're the one that's gonna miss out if you don't come check it out!"

Jasper looked as if he was about to respond sarcastically but then wasn't quite sure what to say. He let his jaw slowly drop open and raised his eyebrows in faked amazement.

"You're such a freak sometimes," Jonathon puffed out in disgust as he shoved his locker door closed and then swung back around to stare down Jasper. "You better be at my house after school. No excuses," he said, giving Jasper an evil eye.

Jasper stared back while contemplating what his fate might be if he did allow Jonathon the pleasure of torturing him with his Dream Machine. For ten long seconds, they relentlessly exchanged glares. Finally, Jasper reached up and clinched Jonathon's shoulder, causing Jonathon to tense up with anticipation.

"You're building Dream Machines and I am the freak?" Jasper didn't lose eye contact as he slowly rolled out the next sentence. "I'll…stop…by."

"Not just stop by…" Jonathon started.

"I'll…stop…by," Jasper interrupted, enunciating each word again, very slowly and carefully. "No other promises."

Jonathon took in a long slow sigh. What else could he do? He knew this probably was a difficult concept for his best friend to grasp. "Let's go to class," he ended up saying as he nodded to let Jasper know he was willing to concede.

The entire day was rather drab, especially knowing he had no chance of running into Leana. On his walk home, he did encounter Kate and had to listen to her ranting about having to babysit an "out-of-control" four-year-old nephew on an upcoming weekend. He'd heard a few of her horror stories before and kind of felt sorry for her. It seemed she was the nice, lovable auntie who wasn't old enough to have a good enough excuse to get out of the torturous task, and too frequently was subjected to "little Dillan's" mischievous ways. Hoping to create an excuse for the next time her older brother asked her to watch Dillan, she planned to look for a "real" job soon.

When Jonathon got to his front door, he was greeted by Lulu exiting with her reusable grocery bags in hand, about to leave for the market.

"Jasper's upstairs, he got here about 25 minutes ago and wanted to wait in your room." She scrambled past Jonathon toward her faded pink 1975 VW Bug parked on the street. Jonathon stood frozen for a moment, soaking in the fact that Jasper was already upstairs, likely checking out the Machine. "You want anything special from the store?" Lulu called out before climbing into her car.

"No thanks!" he hollered rather harshly as he scrambled inside, flinging the front door shut.

He flew up the stairs and became a little miffed to find his bedroom door closed. He barged in as Jasper jumped at the abruptness of Jonathon's entry.

"Hey…" Jasper nervously spewed and then let out a big sigh.

Jonathon eyed Jasper sitting on the edge of his bed. He glanced over to the Machine still covered with a red, white and blue afghan his grandmother had crocheted. He noticed the afghan was a little jostled away on one corner rather than being completely over the device, and the earphone cord previously plugged into the machine was loosely unwound and sticking out from under the blanket. Jonathon thought he had completely covered everything before he left but was now questioning himself. He set his books on his desk and plopped into the chair, thinking he was just being paranoid.

"You got here fast," Jonathon muttered, sounding more as a question than a statement.

"Ya, well, you got here slow," Jasper mocked.

Jonathon felt an uneasiness in the room and decided he should just get down to business. "So, you want to see the Machine?"

Jasper let his next words out in a slow drawl. "I don't know about this." He flung himself backwards from the sitting position onto the bed and let out another huge sigh.

"What the heck's wrong with you? This is the simplest thing in the world! I can program it so you can dream about whatever you want! What's so bad about that?" He waited for a response but continued when he didn't get one. "So what if you dream about something? It's not reality. You're just a huge chicken!"

Jasper got up and grabbed his backpack. "I gotta go."

Jonathon wanted to try to stop Jasper but squashed the temptation and instead slammed the door behind his friend. It was his turn to fling himself onto the bed in frustration. All he wanted was someone else he could trust to validate his Machine worked. *Some friend!* he thought. Anger clouded his brain and the longer he sat, the more perturbed he became. Though it wasn't in his usual nature to be mean, at this moment he really wanted to play a practical joke on Jasper just to teach him a lesson. He jumped up from his bed and went to his desk. The student directory he'd had out the day before was lying there half open, along with the elementary drawing of his Machine he'd sketched a few days prior. He folded the drawing in half and shoved it aside, hoping Lulu hadn't seen it.

Picking up the directory, he flipped to a random page that listed all the faculty. Closing his eyes, he let his finger drop to the middle of the page—Mr. Anthony Mercado.

Jonathon was in his Spanish class. He was a middle-aged, somewhat good-looking Spanish teacher at Cascadia High who most students knew and liked. Although Jonathon had way too much homework to waste time on such things, he went online to do a little research and image searching for his teacher. Jonathon figured it would be harmless to program a little dream about Mr. Mercado for his less-than-helpful friend Jasper to enjoy. He no longer wanted to give Jasper a dream Jasper *wanted*. Jonathon snickered as he sunk down into his chair and pulled out his books to begin studying. *Somehow, I'll get Jasper to cooperate.*

Little did Jonathon know that it was too late. Jasper had seen Jonathon's sketch displaying its simple operation and had already tried out the machine on his own.

Jonathon woke up to the sound of rain against his bedroom window, thankful he had been able to program and save multiple dreams into his Machine. He smiled as he remembered a very vivid dream of Leana. The two were on a boat on the small lake just a few miles outside of town. They were giggling and laughing with flirtatious gestures. He couldn't really recall what they were talking about, only that he had asked her to the school dance, and she seemed delighted.

He sat up on the side of the bed and sighed, thinking it was an awesome dream, but still JUST a dream. Leana had her boyfriend and would never say yes if Jonathon asked her to the dance. Besides, he knew he didn't have the nerve to ask. Contemplating how he was to compete with JR for Leana's affections, Jonathon wrote down on a piece of paper JOIN GYM. Although he had never had a problem with weight, he figured he may as well try to build up his muscles and get into shape.

Jonathon now had his driver's license, having recently turned 16. During his time with a learner's permit, his mother let him drive her to and from the market but only after he'd maneuvered certain skills in a vacant parking lot. Living less than a mile from his high school, he seldom needed to drive. Only when it was raining did he get thrown the keys to his mother's Range Rover, and that was only if she didn't need to go out for the day. He hoped today would be one of those days. Taking her car was a nice, fun break from walking and gave him the needed practice before being allowed to drive further distances.

Lulu was the only one greeting him in the kitchen on this colder-than-average morning.

"How's things?" she asked as she unloaded a small stack of steaming hot pancakes onto Jonathon's plate. Her delicious hot breakfasts always tasted especially good on rainy days.

He knew exactly what "things" she was referring to. Though it had been a few months since she had first learned about his affection for Leana, her prying little questions about his love interest when his parents weren't around kept her up to date. Jonathon appreciated her sensitivity to his privacy by never probing too deeply and loved their relationship. Lulu loved knowing she had a special, maternal-type friendship with her "Jon-Jon."

"Nothing new, Lulu, sorry," he said, offering an apology for his lack of exciting news.

"I really need to get in and do some deep cleaning in your room. Since I can't walk to the market in the rain today, would today be a good time to..."

"No! I mean...I don't think it's a good time right now, Lulu," Jonathon interrupted. He began to sweat, anxious she might find his Machine.

Lulu noticed his reaction and knew his perspiration wasn't from the temperature in the house. "I won't touch your stuff." She then saw him blotting at his forehead with his napkin.

"Well...I might just move it a little to dust..."

"NO! It really doesn't need to be done today, does it? I'd kinda like to straighten up a little first...you know...I have lots of important papers and...and I have a science project that I don't want anyone to mess with." Jonathon spat out excuse after excuse as Lulu stood with her hand on her hip, looking down at him squirming in his seat.

Hesitating before deciding to give Jonathon a comfortable moment to compose himself, Lulu smacked her hand down softly on the table next to his plate and leaned in close. They were eye to eye. "All right then. It is supposed to rain tomorrow, too. Do you suppose you can 'clean up' for me by tomorrow?" She gave a suspicious grin before batting her eyelashes at him in a mocking way.

Jonathon started to blurt out another excuse when he realized it'd just be better if he let her go ahead and do her job. "Fine. I'll straighten up. And I will put a blanket over my science project if you promise to not touch it. It doesn't need dusting and it might ruin it if you move it."

Lulu lifted her hand slowly off the table and placed it back on her rotund hip as she straightened up. Jonathon could tell she was deeply curious about his project.

"When is this science project due? Is it for a science fair? What is it?" Lulu pried.

"Uh…it's just a machine I am building. It, um, it is programmed with information from my classes, so I can listen and study while relaxing." Jonathon then abruptly dove headfirst into his plate of pancakes, shoveling in bites and hoping his mouth would be too full to answer if she asked more.

"Oh, I see. So, it's not for a science class? Just for yourself?" she murmured as she turned to head back to the stove to retrieve a few pieces of bacon for Jonathon.

"Ya. It's nothing really. I mean…it is…I just don't want anyone messing with it. It has a lot of important information in it. Wouldn't want to lose that information. You get it…right?"

Lulu smiled and gave him a wink. "Got it. Tomorrow then."

"Tomorrow." Jonathon acknowledged reluctantly before inhaling the last bites on his plate.

After breakfast, Jonathon ran upstairs to his room to quickly set up his Machine, with hopes he'd convince Jasper to come over again. It took only five minutes to have the dream about Mr. Mercado all ready to go. Jonathon contemplated a moment, wondering if there could be any harmful effects by pulling this prank on his friend. *Am I being too malicious?* he briefly speculated and wondered if this joke might be going a little too far. After all, Jasper hadn't done anything wrong, really. He had always had free admittance to come into Jonathon's room any time over their several years of friendship. He then began thinking his plan was a stupid idea. Pulling from his closet shelf the red, white and blue afghan his grandmother made for him, he covered his Machine, figuring he had all day to think about it. If he changed his mind, he'd delete the dream later. Then he scribbled, PLEASE DON'T TOUCH, on a notecard and paper-clipped it to the yarn of the afghan.

Although Lulu promised she wouldn't clean until the following day, she frequently entered his room to deliver a fresh stack of folded laundry to his dresser or to make his bed on days when Jonathon lazily forgot that chore. Today, he wanted to make sure she knew his machine was off-limits. So, he made his bed and tidied up, giving her less reason to hang around if she did come into his room for any reason.

Jonathon was very happy when his mom did offer him her car. The wind was howling as he drove to school, with brief downpours flooding his vision, making the windshield wipers work at high speed. Once he arrived safe and made his way inside, Jonathon removed his jacket, shaking off the last remaining drops of rain as he scanned the hall. Jasper was nowhere to be seen in either direction. Jonathon waited a few minutes, but he half expected Jasper wouldn't show at their locker this morning. When he entered Mr. Bramble's class, Jasper was in a back corner chair, surrounded by occupied seats. He hadn't saved a seat for him as usual, indicating to Jonathon that Jasper wanted to keep his distance.

Throughout class, Jonathon had some time to think about things and was starting to calm down. By the end of the period, he really began having regrets about his initial vindictiveness toward Jasper. *It really isn't up to Jasper to be the guinea pig in my experiment.* Jonathon decided to give his friend a break and planned to apologize once he got the chance. *I don't need Jasper's help anyway*, he thought, but wished his friend hadn't acted so strange about it.

After class, Jonathon quickly exited the room and waited outside for Jasper to come out. When Jasper finally appeared looking rather nervous, Jonathon grabbed his shoulder to slow him down and hoped to give the apology. Jasper twitched his shoulder to sluff off Jonathon's grasp and started to say something, but Jonathon interrupted.

"Let me talk." He paused, making sure he had Jasper's attention before continuing. "I'm sorry. You don't have to do a thing with my Machine! Okay?"

Jasper heaved a giant sigh. "Thank you." Then he started to walk away.

"Wait…are you still going to be mad? I meant what I said." Jasper stopped and looked to be pondering how he wanted to respond. When Jasper simply stood there without saying anything, Jonathon tried to lighten the conversation. "I had the idea that we should call my Machine a name, you know, so when we're talking about it...no one else knows what we're talking about. What do you think?"

Jasper turned to look at Jonathon but then glanced past Jonathon's shoulder and abruptly lowered his eyes to look at the ground. Jonathon noticed his friend's dark complexion suddenly turning a shade of crimson. Bewildered, Jonathon turned to look behind him and noticed Leana walking past them, practically brushing both of their arms in the crowded hall. She was talking to a friend and made no notice of either of them but Jasper looked abashed. Jonathon was surprised to see her at school at all after what her mother had told him.

"What's going on with you?" Jonathon muttered quietly under his breath.

"Nothing. I…I gotta get to class. See ya later." And with that Jasper turned and rushed off.

Jonathon stood watching his friend until he was just a blur in the sea of students. He felt puzzled by Jasper's odd behavior but decided to not press the matter. He would just let his friend mull over whatever was bothering him.

When Jonathon got to the Study Hall area, he noticed Leana sitting across the room at a table with JR, as usual. She glanced up from her studies as Jonathon walked by and they exchanged quick smiles, giving Jonathon a momentary thrill. He hurried past to find an empty table to unload his backpack before heading up to the snack bar. Dark clouds and treetops tussling in the wind could be seen through the large windows lining the far wall of the large study hall, giving the room a cold, dreary feel. He decided a hot mocha sounded appropriate for such a day. While waiting for his order, he pulled out his phone to avoid looking in the direction of Leana's group of friends. He was standing near the pick-up counter scrolling through e-mails when he felt a soft tap on his shoulder. He turned around, taking a step backwards in surprise when Leana poked her head around the pole.

"Hi," she smiled shyly and then glanced back over her shoulder at the table where JR was seated to observe him watching her every move.

"Hi, Leana." Jonathon, too, looked JR's way nervously but then quickly turned back toward Leana.

"Um, so if you wouldn't mind…I'm going to be leaving in a few minutes to go home. I'm going to need notes for chemistry from yesterday and today's classes…maybe for the whole week…I guess you heard. My mom said you ran into her and know about my…"

"Hey, oh ya, she told me about your grandfather. I'm really sorry." Jonathon wished he could give her a hug as her brow tightened into a painfully, sad look. He might have considered doing so if JR was not in the same room.

"Thanks, Jon." She took a deep sigh and continued. "For starters, do you think I could borrow your notes from yesterday so I can copy them?"

Jonathon led Leana over to his table to retrieve his backpack. As he was reaching in to get his chemistry notebook, an idea popped into his head. He set his backpack back down. "So…I just remembered I was in the middle of rewriting them last night. I think I left them at home. Do you want to come by this weekend to pick them up? I'll just scan all the notes I have for the week and have them ready for you." She was biting her lip and didn't immediately answer, so Jonathon rushed to encourage her. "That way I can explain anything you might not understand."

Leana turned to glance again at JR, noticing he now seemed less interested in what she was doing and was chatting with the group surrounding him. She turned quickly back to Jonathon. "Okay, that's fine. Just text me your address before Saturday. She reached in her purse and grabbed her phone. What's your number? I'll text you so you'll have mine."

Jonathon recited his number, watching her delicate fingers punch them into her phone. He felt his own phone vibrate in his pocket as her text came through. With a quick word of thanks, she dashed back over to her table.

Jonathon hadn't thought an excuse to get Leana to come over would so easily fall into his lap. He now truly needed to rewrite his notes, so he wouldn't look like a liar. Plus, he needed to figure out how he was going to introduce her to his Machine.

When his name was called to retrieve his drink, Jonathon took the opportunity to walk past Leana and JR's table. Out of the corner of his eye he could see and hear them arguing. Leana then grabbed her purse before scrambling off alone in the direction of the exit. Jonathon longed to follow her, but he now had her number and would be contacting her later anyway. Thinking ahead toward the weekend, he was feeling more and more confident it was going to be a good one.

Later during Spanish class as Jonathon sat watching Mr. Mercado scribble notes on the board, he thought to himself what a stupid idea it was to program his Machine with dreams about his teacher. It was simply an impulsive idea meant as a backlash toward his best friend. But Jonathon was beginning to realize Jasper didn't deserve *any* sort of retaliation, so he made the decision to re-program his Machine as soon as he got home. He missed talking with his best friend.

There was no sign of Jasper as Jonathon was leaving the school. He was hoping to see him and offer him a ride. However, he did see Kate walking briskly down the street in her raincoat when he was about to turn the corner toward his house. She began waving when she saw him slow down. He pulled over and rolled down the passenger window, glad the rain had slowed to a sprinkle.

Kate leaned in through the open window. "Glad I caught you. Didn't see you much today."

Jonathon let out a breathy laugh. "Sorry I didn't see you sooner. I would have offered you a ride."

Kate waved it off like it was no big deal. "You're not supposed to drive others yet anyway."

"Right," he rolled his eyes. "Anyway, today was kind of weird," Jonathon huffed. "Jasper's a little ticked about something. He'll get over it but I didn't hang around my locker much. Giving him some space."

"Why? What's he mad about?" She leaned on her elbow through the open window.

"Oh…it's nothing. What are you up to this weekend?" Jonathon started to ask but then remembered her plans. "Oh…forgot…you're babysitting."

Kate gave him a bitter look, as if it was his fault. "Certainly not looking forward to it!"

"You'd better hurry and get that other job you talked about!" Jonathon said jokingly.

"It's hardly a laughing matter! My mom told me the bookstore on Juniper Street and Main has a sign posted on their window for help. I was waiting until after the dance to apply in case they want me to start right away...that's if I get the job."

"Well, you'd better hurry before someone else applies and gets it. Just tell them you aren't available until...when is the dance, again?"

"A week from Saturday. Ya...I will probably go by there Sunday if I have any energy left after taking care of that little..." Kate let her remark trail off and she rolled her eyes.

"Okay. Well, hope you have a good night. Better rest up! You'll need your energy," Jonathon laughed.

Kate gave him the stink eye, even knowing he was just teasing. "Well, good luck with Jasper." She gave the car door a little pat and with a wink she turned to continue her walk home.

When Jonathon walked in the door to his house, Lulu was coming down the stairs toward the entrance hall. Jonathon greeted her but Lulu didn't even look up. She was carrying a basket of laundry. "Leave your wet shoes right there at the door," she muttered as she turned the corner and headed toward the laundry room. "There's cookies in the kitchen," she stated flatly.

Jonathon did as he was told and slipped off his Vans. Not hungry, he ignored the cookie offer and trudged up the stairway. He needed to re-program his machine right away and start in on his homework. At this point, he had assignments in every one of his classes. When he walked into his room, he immediately looked toward his Machine and his heart sank when he noticed the afghan covering it seemed a little misplaced. He felt sure he had covered it completely by putting the knitted blanket squarely across it.

Surveying the room, he didn't see any other sign of disruption. When Lulu cleaned, he normally noticed pictures and knickknacks slightly moved from dusting, along with a lingering fresh smell of Lemon Pledge. Nothing else was out of place. She had promised not to clean until tomorrow, so Jonathon was hoping she had only peeked under the blanket out of curiosity.

Closing the door behind him, Jonathon went to his Machine and pulled off the afghan. As he did, he noticed that the sign he had pinned to it was now on the back side. He had forgotten about the DO NOT TOUCH sign. Someone, likely Lulu, HAD moved it or had been prying. His parents rarely came in his room but if it was one of them, they'd later ask him about his project.

Feeling he shouldn't worry about it, Jonathon plopped down in his desk chair for a moment and decided to conjure up another dream for that night. The sketch he'd drawn of his Machine sat flattened out, laying on top a stack of books. *I could have sworn I folded it in half.*

He didn't feel in the mood but needed to erase the dream about Mr. Mercado. He opened his computer to locate the dream file currently playing and hit delete. *No need in keeping that dream,* he thought. After a few moments, he came up with a replacement dream where he and Leana were sitting in his room laughing and eating some of Lulu's delicious monster cookies. Massaging his temples, Jonathon was simply too tired to think of anything more creative. His eyelids kept closing and he struggled to stay awake. Unable to focus, he decided the short dream was sufficient. It only took him less than 10 minutes to complete the reprograming.

Hesitantly, he pulled out his chemistry notes and began rewriting them. His mind drifted and his eyelids started to flutter once again. Fighting to stay awake, he began thinking about how dreams are linked to something called Rapid Eye Movement (also known as R.E.M.). He whispered it out loud, "REM." He said it again slowly and added a Y. "REMY." That was it! He perked up and quickly wrote REMY in capital letters below the drawing of his Machine. The name seemed perfect! He didn't even reconsider the decision, feeling excitement and relief to finally have a nickname.

Hearing and feeling his stomach growl, Jonathon figured Lulu's mention of cookies must have been the trigger, so he headed downstairs hoping for a snack. The break would also help him stay awake for at least a little while longer. Down in the kitchen, Lulu stood at the sink peeling potatoes. She seemed unusually quiet. Jonathon walked over to help himself to the cookie jar and was not disappointed, finding a fresh batch of Snickerdoodles. He wrapped a couple of them in a napkin and grabbed a soda from the refrigerator. Lulu didn't seem in any mood for chit chat, so Jonathon headed back upstairs. He definitely thought from the way she was acting that she had been the one snooping around his room and was now feeling guilty.

Jonathon caught up on his assignments and even did a little research for the upcoming chemistry project, so he would have more to contribute to Leana on the weekend. By the time he was supposed to go down for dinner, he felt drained. Sauntering down the stairs once again, he entered the kitchen to find his father alone, pouring himself a glass of iced tea.

"Where is mom…and Lulu?" Jonathon asked.

"Hello to you too," Jonathon's dad sarcastically addressed his son as he stood struggling to break out ice cubes from a silicone tray. "Lulu said she didn't feel well and retreated to her room to get a good night's sleep. Your mother is at a book club meeting."

"Sorry," Jonathon apologized feeling disrespectful. "How was your day, dad?"

His father cleared his throat as he went to sit at the table. "Just fine." Jonathon waited, expecting a lecture but none came. His father had seemed moody lately and today was no exception. Jonathon decided to let his dad be the first to start a conversation, just in case he wasn't in a good mood. While waiting, he reflected on the past few months. His parents rarely did much together anymore. When they were both at home, each of them usually seemed absorbed in their separate projects.

Dinner was neatly situated on the table, arranged by Lulu in covered dishes on a warming plate. Jonathon began dishing up helpings of Lulu's favorite standby meal for the two of them, beef empanadillas. His father eventually started talking about the stock market, but then threw in a story about his golf buddy, Joe, who had recently got a hole in one. As Jonathon ate his dinner, nodding and trying to act interested in his father's stories, all he could think about was going to bed.

When they had finished eating, Jonathon excused himself from the table and returned to his room to text Jasper. He gave his friend another apology and texted that he'd see him tomorrow. After several minutes he got a reply from Jasper that read, "**CU**

tomorrow," with a thumbs-up emoji. Tomorrow couldn't come soon enough, thought Jonathon; *everyone is so weird today.*

Six

The following morning, Jonathon woke to a surprise. He had forgotten to hook himself up to his Machine before bed. In fact, he had been so exhausted he'd fallen asleep in his clothes. But he did remember having a dream during the night about being at a zoo with Leana. Even though the details were foggy, he wondered if this meant REMY left lasting imprints on his brain from the prior use. And if so, perhaps he would continue to dream about Leana without having to hook himself up to his Machine every single night.

Lying in his bed, he listened to the clink-clink-clink of rain-drops hitting the rain-gutter outside his window. It was coming down soft and steady, almost lulling him back to sleep. When he finally dragged himself up, he threw on a pair of sweats and plodded down to the kitchen. This time he was greeted by his mom who sat sipping her morning coffee and reading something on her iPad. Lulu was at the sink washing dishes.

"Morning, Johnny." She tilted her head down to look at him over her bifocals, then grinned as if she had a secret. "Your dad told me you might be going to a school dance."

Jonathon was glad to hear that his mom and dad did talk on occasion. "Morning, mom." He smiled back warily as he sat down in front of a plate of avocado toast. "I am thinking about it. No big deal." He saw his mom give an endearing glance Lulu's way as Lulu reciprocated the gesture.

"Well, I think that's a great idea. You seem so busy and preoccupied in your room lately. You need to get out and socialize," his mother told him, warmly conveying her concern.

Jonathon had the impulse to defend his recent behavior but decided against saying anything. He didn't want to lie or invite more questions. "Can I please have a cup of coffee, Lulu?" Lulu obliged but still seemed to avoid making eye contact with Jonathon.

Mrs. Samuels continued with morning chitchat, letting Jonathon know of her day's plans. She picked up the creamer and added a little to her cup. As she stirred her coffee, she was going on and on as if she hadn't seen her son in weeks. He tried to listen patiently but his thoughts got sidetracked thinking of his own plans for the day.

"Since it's raining and you need a car, I need you to drop Lulu off at the market this morning on your way to school," his mom pleaded. "I will get your father to pick her up before he heads to work. Her car is in the shop getting new brakes." Lulu turned and looked like she was about to protest but then stopped herself.

"Sure," Jonathon mumbled with his mouth now full. He glanced up at Lulu who had since turned back around. His mom gave him a smile of thanks and indicated with her pinky finger where he needed to wipe off a smudge of avocado clinging to the side of his lip.

Mrs. Samuels then retreated to her bedroom. When Jonathon finished, he told Lulu he'd be down and ready to go in about 20 minutes. She kept her back to him and acknowledged with a grumble. He stood staring at her back for a moment. Then he slowly shook his head and rolled his eyes before dashing upstairs. He needed to finish getting ready and to wrap his Machine in plastic and duct tape before her threatened cleaning of his room. Straightening up his desk, he made sure to tuck his sketch of REMY with the stick person in a drawer.

When Jonathon got back downstairs, Lulu was standing ready in her floral raincoat with an umbrella. She had the look of a guilty little kid on her face.

"You ready to go?" Jonathon asked her even though the answer was obvious.

"Yes Jon-Jon. Thanks for taking me." She turned to follow him.

Jonathon opened the door leading to the garage and motioned for her to go first. "Is everything okay, Lulu?" He knew her moods, but this was a new one to him. Usually, she would be chit-chatty and asking questions about everything under the sun.

"What do you mean?" she walked past and into the garage, giving him a defensive look.

"You seem like something's wrong this morning..." Jonathon followed her to the car with raised eyebrows and opened the passenger door. "…ever since yesterday when I got home from school."

"Nothing is wrong. Don't be silly, Jon-Jon.!" Lulu raised her head up tall to emphasize her statement as a fact before sliding into the seat. "I plan to clean your room today, okay? Do you remember I am planning to do that today?" Lulu threw out these questions without even looking at Jonathon. He slipped into the driver's seat without answering and as he backed the car out, she kept her head turned away from him, looking out her window. "Because I want to make sure it's okay to go in your room before I do," she blurted out while the car sat idling in the driveway as Jonathon fidgeted with the garage door button

It seemed strange she was making a big deal about it, he thought. "Yeah, I picked up a little. Feel free to clean away." He chuckled, trying to lighten the air. "Just please don't bother with REMY." As he said it, he realized she wouldn't know what he is talking about. "That's my Machine's name," he added.

With that, Lulu's head spun around abruptly toward Jonathon. "I won't!" she quipped, but then bit her lip quickly, trying to hide her reaction. "I mean, good. That I can clean." She turned once again to look out her window. "Where did you get *that* name?"

Jonathon splayed one hand away from the driving wheel and shrugged his shoulders. He wasn't in the mood to explain. "I have my reasons," he quipped, now feeling slightly irritated with her.

"Of course, you do, Jon-Jon." Lulu looked at him lovingly and finally gave a little grin.

In less than 10 minutes, Jonathon was pulling into Grocer's Corner to drop off Lulu. He pulled into a parking spot right in front, so she could dash inside without getting soaked from the steady rain.

"Okay, I guess dad will pick you up in a bit. You have your phone to call him?" Jonathon asked thoughtfully.

"Yes, Jon-Jon," Lulu was saying when she suddenly let out an exasperated gasp and slid down in her seat to lower her head from view.

Jonathon flinched and grabbed Lulu's shoulder. "Are you all right? What's wrong Lulu?" Jonathon's breathing sped up with anxiety over what was happening. He looked out the front window wondering if there was anyone around to help him, thinking she might need medical aid. That's when he saw his Spanish teacher, Mr. Mercado, standing on the sidewalk in front of the store with a bag tucked under his coat for protection from the rain. Mr. Mercado didn't notice Jonathon, but instead was fumbling with an umbrella and seemed to be looking for his car or for someone picking him up.

Lulu grabbed Jonathon's sleeve and tugged. "Don't look at him, Jon-Jon!" Jonathon peered down at Lulu quizzically, noticing her eyes fixated over the dash of the car and onto Mr. Mercado.

"What's going on, Lulu? Do you know Mr. Mercado?" Jonathon probed Lulu as she remained sunken on the car floor.

"I never saw him before in my life. You know him?" Lulu's eyes followed Mr. Mercado as he sprang from the curb in the rain, jogging past their car toward the parking lot.

Jonathon watched Lulu with his mouth agape. "He's my Spanish teacher, Lulu."

She quickly straightened up and tried to compose herself. Her entire face looked rosy beneath her dark Filipino complexion. She grabbed the car door handle and moaned "Sorry Jon-Jon…I'm okay." She looked absolutely frazzled. "That is your Spanish teacher?"

Jonathon nodded his head slowly as she then turned to rush out, slamming the door behind her. He sat in a stupor as he watched her run into the market.

Jonathon muttered to himself, "What the heck just happened?" *How strange*, he thought as he put the car into reverse. He was pulling out onto the street, rehashing what had just occurred when he felt a growing pit in his stomach. Beginning to realize the potential cause for Lulu's odd behavior made him feel panicky. *She must have been messing around with my Machine the day before…to a greater extent than I feared! Could she have somehow hooked herself up to REMY and intercepted the dream about Mr. Mercado, having ignored the "Don't Touch" sign?*

Jonathon was imagining Lulu finding his drawing and using it to hook herself up to REMY. He couldn't fathom her being so nosy or bold. However, the drawing illustrated its use simply, he thought. This would explain why the blanket was on backwards…and why she seemed so uncomfortable around Jonathon this morning. He began speculating she might be feeling guilty for betraying him and meddling with his "science project."

The entire scenario started to seem comical, and he began chuckling. Suddenly, a loud horn honking shook him from his own reckless daydreaming as he realized he was about to run a red light. Jonathon slammed on the brakes, causing the car to skid on the wet pavement before bringing the car to a screeching halt just past the crosswalk. He let out a long, slow sigh and tried to back up a little while getting nasty stares from the few pedestrians rushing across in the rain. Once the light changed and he got through the intersection, he pulled over to the side of the road to calm down and gain his composure. Taking another deep breath, he let out a bellowing sound of frustration as he made a pact with himself to not be as careless with REMY in the future.

Jonathon was happy to make it to school safely after the chaotic morning. However, Jasper continued to display the oddest behavior toward him during their first period class. Jonathon wanted to tell Jasper about the morning and about Lulu, but he'd then have to tell him of his plan to prank him with the dream about Mr. Mercado. Instead, Jonathon kept quiet, and they had little interaction. Thankfully, study hall period was uneventful. In fact, Leana was nowhere to be seen and JR was just hanging out with a bunch of guys. Jonathon took full advantage of the time to focus and catch up on more homework.

When chemistry rolled around, Leana was still absent, so he assumed she was not at school at all. The distraction of having her in class had been taking a toll on him and he found it relaxing to simply do his work and take notes without her presence.

At the start of lunch, Jonathon was at his locker and didn't notice Jasper approaching. Jasper didn't slap his buddy on the back, as usual, and instead flung his arm over the locker door, hanging on it like an old coat. "So, I see Leana isn't here today."

Jonathon flinched at Jasper's statement, then stood up straight, cocking his head slightly with amusement. "Are you taking roll now?" He thought it was an odd observation made by his friend. *Since when has Jasper ever care about Leana being at school?*

Jasper released the locker door and pulled his shoulders back with a defensive stance. "I just noticed she isn't here! Thought you'd want to know!" he barked. With that he turned around and strutted off down the hall.

Jonathon laughed and looked around, half wondering if he was getting punked. *What was his problem?* he thought. He slammed the locker door and set off to grab a bite in the cafeteria. He was glad the weekend was almost here. He'd had enough drama this week and although he felt a bit nervous, he was looking forward to having Leana come to his house.

After lunch, Jonathon entered Spanish class. He snickered when the first thing he noticed was his teacher's soggy umbrella propped by the door with a damp ring below it on the carpet. Mr. Mercado was writing Spanish phrases on the chalkboard. As Jonathon walked past, he saw a half-eaten muffin sitting on a flattened bag from Grocer's Corner, sitting on the corner of his desk. Jonathon turned and made his way down an aisle, then slithered into a seat. He felt certain Mr. Mercado hadn't noticed him and Lulu in the car earlier and knew his teacher had no idea what transpired. A few minutes before the bell, Kate rushed in and grabbed one of the only seats left at the front of the class. She mouthed something to Jonathon but he couldn't understand her. He shrugged, so she turned back around to face the front.

Mr. Mercado began the class going over topics each student could choose from to give a speech in Spanish, as part of their mid-terms. Jonathon was listening intently to the instructions being given when Susan Shooflee, who was seated behind Kate but across the aisle from Jonathon, turned around and thrust her hand out toward Jonathon. She was passing a note from Kate and did nothing to hide the transaction. Jonathon grabbed it from her hand just as Mr. Mercado turned from the blackboard toward the class. Their teacher noticed something was going on but only paused and lifted his chiseled chin up as if looking through bifocals and stared the two of them down for a few seconds before continuing his lesson.

Jonathon threw an annoyed look across the aisle toward Susan who then returned a smug grin. Because he was now under a watchful eye, Jonathon didn't even try to look at the note until class was nearly over. When the bell was about to ring Jonathon opened the folded paper:

Can I come over tomorrow and interview you for the school paper? I am writing about the debate team.

T*hat's just great*, Jonathon thought, crumpling the note in his hand. Waiting for the bell, he tried to quickly decide what he should tell Kate. He didn't yet know what time Leana was coming.

As soon as class was dismissed, Kate rushed back to Jonathon's seat.

"Sorry for the short notice, but I have to have an article by Monday! They want something about the debate team. I knew I could count on you." She spoke, without thinking for a second that he might be busy. She was digging through her backpack and not looking at Jonathon.

"I kinda have plans. Can we do it tonight?" Jonathon responded.

Kate's mouth dropped. "Nooooo! I have to babysit tonight, remember?!" she quipped, annoyed at her own situation. "What are you doing tomorrow? Are you busy all day?" She seemed to have found whatever she was looking for in her backpack and was now staring directly into his eyes.

Jonathon felt his face heating up. For some reason, he was embarrassed to tell her what he was doing. Kate had no idea about REMY, and certainly didn't know about his intentions to use it on Leana. In fact, she had no idea Jonathon had any feelings toward Leana at all. "I am just meeting a friend…well, a friend is coming by to get some notes for chemistry class. Not sure what time yet but I may have to help her with deciphering my notes."

Kates's eyebrows lifted and she gave a quizzical expression showing off her dimples. "Her?"

Jonathon squirmed, realizing his blunder. "It's just Leana. She has been gone from class because her grandfather passed." Kate nodded with a long face at the affirmation of this news. "I'm just being nice and letting her look at my notes. I'd let her copy them, but she'll never be able to make out my writing. I probably need to help her figure them out."

Jonathon wasn't used to lying about anything, but it seemed to be a growing habit lately. Sweat beads began to form on his forehead and he used the end of his sleeve to casually dab them as he waited for Kate's reaction.

Seeing Jonathon's uneasiness, Kate furrowed her forehead. "O...K...I can work around whatever timing...that is, if you don't mind me interviewing you. I'm just kind of in a pinch."

"Sure." Jonathon took a deep breath, dabbing his brow again. "It's warm in here," he chuckled.

Kate, likewise, took a deep breath and scrunched her mouth in a perplexing grin, not quite buying all that Jonathon was telling her. "Text me a time...okay? I'll try to stay un-busy so I can run over when it's good for you...that is, if I survive babysitting tonight." She turned to walk out of class but gave one last glance over her shoulder at Jonathon. He was watching her and praying she wouldn't mess up his plans with Leana. She was thinking Jonathon's odd behavior made her wish she could be a fly on his bedroom wall tomorrow during Leana's visit.

As soon as school let out, Jonathon went straight to his car, threw his stuffed backpack in the backseat, and removed his dampened jacket. It was still lightly raining, so he quickly slithered onto the driver's seat and took a deep breath before searching on his phone for Leana's text. He read the one line she'd sent. **Hi. It's Leana.** He smiled reading it, then created a new contact with her name and number. After careful consideration, he chose her ringtone to be a constellation sound. Not remembering if he was supposed to call her or if she was to call him, he settled on the safe side and texted her.

Hey Leana. Jon here. 😉 Didn't see you today…do you still want to stop by for the Chem notes?

He read the text before hitting 'send' and decided to take out the emoji. Then he laid the seat back a little and felt a warm ray of sun hitting the side of his face. It was coming in the side window, peeking through a small break in the clouds. Hoping he might spot a rainbow, he kept his focus on the sky through the Range Rover's sunroof. Within a minute, the sun disappeared, eliminating that possibility. He checked his phone again. Still no message so he closed his eyes, feeling annoyed. *Don't girls live on their phones?* He decided to head home and wait to hear from her. Pulling out of the school lot, he made a split decision to stop for a smoothie at Yummy Yogurt, so he headed toward the main street in town. One block from school he saw Kate kneeling on the sidewalk up ahead… again, digging in her backpack while struggling to hold her umbrella handle between her chin and shoulder. He slowly pulled over to the curb and rolled down the opposite side window.

"I'm know, I know. I'm not supposed to have passengers yet." Kate put her hand on her chest, startled when Jonathon hollered out the window. "But I think it'd be okay to give you a ride home." He pointed beyond her. "Those clouds over there are getting darker."

"Sure, thanks." Kate reorganized her grip on her backpack, books and cellphone and hopped in the passenger seat, throwing her umbrella onto the floor of the back seat.

"Did you walk to school in the rain this morning?' Jonathon questioned.

"No, my brother gave me a ride. Guess he doesn't want me getting sick and bailing on babysitting duties," she sarcastically chuckled.

Jonathon laughed at Kate seeing humor in the situation. "Well, I was going to stop for a smoothie. You want one?"

"Brrr! No, but I could go for a hot mocha or something," she said rubbing her hands together to warm them up.

Jonathon was wearing a long-sleeved Shetland wool sweater and was quite warm but he took her gesture as a hint and turned up the heater.

"Well, I can get something at the The Coffee Couch. Let's stop there."

Kate gave a big grin and bounced her head in an approving nod. It was a short ride and the two old friends felt comfortable riding in silence. He found a parking spot on the street out in front.

"I'll get it. You can stay here unless you want to go in for a little bit?" The Coffee Couch was true to its name and had several comfortable old couches situated in pods, making it easy for patrons to have conversations. The place had a Bohemian feel and was a warm and inviting place to hang out. It was especially popular with high school students.

"Appreciate it…but…babysitting. Remember?"

Jonathon gave a click with his tongue and a thumbs-up as he was once again reminded.

Walking in, he acknowledged a few kids in line who he knew from school. He scooted past them to the back, looking over their heads to view the coffee menu. Once he placed his order, he walked over to wait in a corner. When he turned around, he spotted Jasper sitting on a barstool at a tall round table in the distance. He was laughing and sipping a coffee drink. Whoever he was with had their back to Jonathon, but he could definitely tell it was a girl by the petite frame. She was wearing a tufted rain jacket with a scarf around her neck and a beanie, which hid her hair. Jonathon started to weave between couches toward them when Jasper suddenly noticed him approaching and almost choked on a gulp of coffee. With that, the girl sitting with him turned to see what Jasper was reacting to.

Jonathon stopped in his tracks for the briefest second when he saw Leana's face. Trying to disguise his exasperation, he slowed his walk, looking at one and then the other, then settling his sight on Jasper as he stopped before them.

"Hey. How's it going?" Jonathon felt nervous being this close to Leana in a setting other than school. But his aggravation with his best friend was over-riding the nerves.

Jasper looked as if he'd seen a ghost. "Hey, Jon." He was fidgeting on the bar stool like there were ants in his pants. "Leana was home today because there are lots of relatives in town for the funeral Sunday. And so, I just asked her if she wanted to get out of the house and have a cocoa or something."

Jonathon gave a look of annoyance to his friend and then turned to look at Leana. He cleared his throat. "I tried texting you about timing for tomorrow." Then he side-eyed his friend to let him know he wasn't happy.

Leana seemed oblivious to the tension in the air. "Sorry...I got the text right as we were getting our coffees. I was going to text you back later." She then gave a smile toward Jasper. "It was nice of Jasper to offer to get me out of the house. I needed a break; it's so crammed with relatives." Jonathon felt annoyed when her grin lingered toward Jasper a few long seconds before she turned to Jonathon.

"That's okay" Jonathon said, but not really meaning it. He was absolutely stumped. *Leana has a boyfriend. Jasper is my best friend and knows how much I have been working on my Machine, and the reason I built REMY in the first place. When did Jasper even get her number?* he wondered. *And here they are enjoying a cozy, little cup of coffee.* "Well, I'll let you two continue on then. Do you still want to come by for the notes?" Jonathon was trying his hardest to not sound perturbed.

"Yes, if that's OK. Is 10:00 or 10:30 good?"

"Sure. I'll see you then." Jonathon turned to leave, giving Jasper a brief, scornful glare once Leana looked away. He normally would give his friend a high five or a friendly boxing punch into his shoulder as a goodbye but he didn't, sending a message to Jasper.

Waiting for the drink order to come up, Jonathon glanced their way a few times. Leana still had her back to Jonathon, but he could tell by her hand movements and tilt of her head she was talking and apparently having a good time. In contrast, Jasper looked tense and serious and met Jonathon's glances a time or two. Jasper knew he would have to answer to him at a later point.

Driving Kate home, Jonathon did not bring up his encounter with Jasper and Leana. He didn't want to reveal his emotions and have her start asking questions. He dropped her off as the rain was starting to lighten up again. "How about just coming by around noon tomorrow if you want that interview?" he offered.

Before closing the door, Kate shot a sweet grin at Jonathon. "You're the best. Thank you. I hope no one saw you driving me. Wouldn't want you to get your license revoked already!"

"Hope you survive the little monster tonight." Jonathon gave his friend a wink. He pulled away toward home, knowing he needed to get to work after dinner to program REMY for Leana's visit. He wanted to have everything in place, so there would be no mistakes in carrying out his plan once Leana arrived. He had been conjuring this up for so long and wanted to feel excited. Instead, he now just felt like he needed to hurry before his best friend ruined his plans.

That night, Jonathon felt exhausted after making small talk at dinner with his family. He had done some of his homework when he first got home from school but still needed to re-write his chemistry notes and program REMY. Lulu seemed back to normal after a brief display of embarrassment, briefly lowering her eyes when Jonathon first walked in the door. Trying to put her at ease, Jonathon had quickly interrogated her about where she was hiding the cookies as he opened and shut several cupboards in a playful manner.

Once he retreated to his room for the night, Jonathon noticed his phone light up with a text from Jasper.

Oh great, he thought. At the moment, he was not in the mood to deal with Jasper's contrite excuses, so he tossed his phone onto his bed without reading the text.

Since his Machine would take a bit more thought and preparation than re-writing notes, Jonathon decided to program REMY first. He pulled out a picture he'd saved of Leana from a chemistry class group photo taken earlier in the year. He scanned the photo and fed it to the machine along with the picture he had of himself. He entered key words like "kiss" and "eye contact" and digitalized a location, which looked similar to the storage room at the back of the chemistry lab. He programmed the popular love song, "Just in Time." He typed in a scenario; they were alone after class and couldn't take their eyes off each other. After fidgeting with all the settings and deciding the machine was ready, he sighed a breath of relief. Throwing himself back on the bed for a few minutes he picked up his phone and opened the three texts he now had from Jasper.

What are you up to tonight? Can we talk?

Okay. I get it. Sorry! She's really nice and I just felt like being a friend.

OK! I can't help it. I can't quit thinking about her! I think it's your fault!!!!!

Jonathon bolted upright. *What does he mean by that?!* He threw the phone back onto the bed and went to work typing his notes instead of re-writing them, feeling like steam was seeping out of his pores as he punched the keys. *Some friend,* he thought! A burst of energy fueled by rage benefitted Jonathon and kept him awake long enough to finish. It had taken an hour and a half, but he now sat at his desk, completely drained, while waiting for the printer to deliver his notes. He then neatly folded the papers and placed them in a pale green envelope, one he earlier found in his mother's desk drawer. He wrote *LEANA* in his best penmanship on the front before carefully tucking it inside his chemistry book.

He proceeded with his nighttime ritual of setting his alarm and plugging his phone into its charger. Another notification flashed across the front of his phone, letting him know he had one more text from Jasper. But Jonathon felt he wouldn't be able to sleep if it was another infuriating explanation, so he muted his phone and turned the screen downward on the desk for the night. Finally, crawling under the warmth of his comforter, he barely laid his head down on the pillow and within a minute he was out. He didn't wake a single moment, until his alarm went off the following morning.

The sun was shining through a small crack in the shutters right onto Jonathon's Machine. As he lay in bed, he gave a smile and gazed proudly at his masterpiece. He felt he'd worked hard to perfect his invention. A nervous excitement was running through his veins. "Time to do what you do best," he spoke out loud to REMY as if his Machine could hear him.

He picked up his phone and found another notification of a text from Leana. His heart almost stopped, fearing she needed to cancel. He quickly opened his phone and went straight to her text. She only wanted to verify their meeting time and his address. Jonathon felt a release of tension from his body as he sent a reply.

Then he opened Jasper's unread text from the previous night.

You're a jerk.

Jonathon leaned back in his chair and combed his hair with his fingers while he sat thinking. He hated the recent strain on his relationship with his best friend and was absolutely stumped as to why Jasper would be pursuing the girl he knew Jonathon had been interested in for several months.

His morning shower helped calm him as he turned the temperature to the highest degree he could tolerate. Letting the heat relax his shoulders, he closed his eyes and began to recall another dream about Leana during the night, but the memory of it was vague. Once he got out, he stood staring at his closet for several minutes. *This must be what Kate means when she says it takes her forever to get ready for special occasions*, he thought.

Before heading downstairs, Jonathon peeked down the hall toward his parents' bedroom. The door was cracked open. He tiptoed softly toward their room as he took in a warm, sweet smell lofting up from the kitchen downstairs. He hoped it was one of Lulu's delicious, homemade baked cinnamon rolls she often made on the weekends.

Poking his head into the master bedroom, he skimmed the room and was relieved to see the bed made and no sign of either parent. It was almost 9:00 a.m. and his parents were typically early-risers. So, feeling safe to enter, he tiptoed across to his father's collection of colognes displayed atop a bureau. Jonathon only owned one bottle of cologne, a recent birthday gift from his aunt. Its fragrance reminded him of a forest, a smell he doubted would incite Leana's affection. He opened and sniffed at a few of the bottles and found one he remembered liking when worn by his father. He dabbed a small bit on his neck and arm and then rushed out, making sure to leave everything looking untouched.

Downstairs, just as Jonathon hoped, Lulu was just pulling a pan of piping hot rolls from the oven. Both of his parents were seated at each end of their farm style dinette table, completely disengaged.

Jonathon lifted his nose high and took in the aroma as he walked over to Lulu who was now topping the loaf with a cream cheese frosting.

"Nothing better than that smell, Lulu," Jonathon complimented his nanny as she stood straight and turned to look up at him with her all-too-common raised eyebrows.

She mouthed a barely whispered, "And…how can you smell anything over that Christian Dior you're wearing?"

Jonathon turned away from the table and faced the oven as if this would keep the cologne smell from wafting toward his parents. He leaned down to whisper to Lulu. "Is it that obvious?"

She elbowed his side. "I'm just teasing you. It's not *that* strong. I just know you don't have any of that fancy stuff." She poked him with the handle of the spatula. "You are so dressed up for a Saturday morning." Her eyes were questioning but he was saved from answering when his father suddenly noticed his son in the room.

"Oh, Jon. Good morning." His father cleared his throat and flipped the page of the morning paper. "You're dressed up awfully nice this morning. What do you have going on today?" With that, his mother also looked up from something she was writing.

Jonathon nervously turned toward his father but stayed his distance, hoping he, too, wouldn't notice the smell of the cologne he had borrowed. "Umm. Well, a friend is stopping by for some chemistry notes this morning and I didn't want to look like a slob."

Lulu used her raised eyebrows again as she kept facing the oven and side-eyed Jonathon with a smirk. "Your girl, Leana?" she said barely loud enough for him to hear.

Jonathon shushed at Lulu but gave her a half-nod.

"Well, that's nice of you. Must not be Jasper," his father joked.

"No, it's just a girl from my chemistry class that needs notes from a couple of days that she missed." With that comment, his mom now seemed more interested in the conversation and set down her pen.

"It's just...it's because she...I mean her grandfather passed away last week and I want to help her out. I mean, I need to..." Jonathon felt tongue-tied and a warmth began crawling up his neck causing his face to flush. "Gosh, it's toasty in here standing over this oven, Lulu. I don't know how you do it all day." Jonathon chuckled nervously, pulling at his shirt collar while trying to mask his embarrassment.

"Well, that's very nice of you, Jon. I wish I was going to be here to meet her," his mother apologized. "I have a ladies' brunch at the golf club this morning. What time is she coming?"

Jonathon noticed his father eyeing his mother over the top of the newspaper with a look of annoyance when she mentioned her brunch. "In about an hour." Jonathon answered while still watching his dad, who kept a smug look on his face as he returned to browsing the paper. Jonathon looked back at his mom. "It's okay. I'm sure she'll just stop by for a few minutes. I just need to explain a few things to her that she might not understand... from the lecture." Jonathon was relieved to know his mother was going to be out of the house.

"I probably will be gone too, Jon. You'll have to offer the kids some tea, Lulu," Jonathon's dad piped in without looking up. *Double bonus*, Jonathon thought. *Both parents gone.* He didn't know how long it might take, or if he would even be able to convince Leana to use his machine. And he wasn't so sure they'd be fine with him inviting her to his bedroom.

Mr. and Mrs. Samuels sat completely quiet, tending to themselves as Jonathon devoured the warm, gooey cinnamon roll Lulu had placed in front of him on the counter where he still stood at a good distance away from his parents

When he finished, he placed his plate in the dishwasher and rinsed his fingers under the kitchen faucet. "You aren't going to sit down?" his mom asked. She stood and walked over to a kitchen drawer and began rummaging through its contents. "Where on earth is the envelope to this card?" she mumbled to herself in apparent frustration. "Lulu, have you seen a light green envelope?"

Jonathon quickly excused himself before she could question him too, saying he needed to straighten his room a bit. He bolted up the stairs, not waiting to hear the results of her search. He already knew she wouldn't find the envelope. It was tucked nicely away in his room with Leana's name on it.

About 15 minutes later, Jonathon breathed a sigh of relief after each of his parents separately pulled out of the driveway and off to their individual plans. He took his phone off vibrate mode and increased the volume, so he wouldn't miss a text or call from Leana. He had never felt so nervous. The anticipation was causing his stomach to hurt. His arms felt weak, and his shoulders were tight as knots. This was unlike anything he'd ever experienced before.

Attempting to shake off the nerves, he put on some music and lay back on his pillow, closing his eyes. A few minutes later, he started wishing he knew something about meditation. He literally felt nauseated by the time his phone made a loud "constellation" tone and he nearly jumped out of his skin.

I **am leaving now. See you in about 15.**

Jonathon stood up to pace the short length of his room. *This is crazy*, he thought. *But what's the worst that can happen?* Fifteen minutes felt like an hour, especially when it turned out to be closer to 30 minutes. He kept going to his window to peak through the shutters. Finally, he decided he'd better let Lulu know he'd be in his room tutoring Leana, hoping she'd take the hint to stay away.

"Whatever you say, Jon-Jon. This is your big chance to make a good impression…am I right?" Lulu grinned. "Do you want me to make you some lemonade or something?"

"I don't think so. She shouldn't be here that long. I…we probably don't want to be disturbed if we are going over notes and I'm not sure how long she can stay."

Lulu did her classic hand on the hip stance while making a stop sign gesture with the other and grinned. "Well, I will make some just in case you change your mind."

The anticipation of the occasion had heightened their senses, so when the doorbell chimed, it startled them both. They froze and looked at each other as if they had just committed a crime. Then Lulu ran her hands quickly down the front of her checkered apron to flatten the wrinkles and did an about-face back into the kitchen.

Jonathon took a deep breath and cleared his throat before heading to the door. "Well, here goes," he muttered to himself.

He tried to act nonchalant as he swung open the heavy, over-sized mahogany door. Leana was standing back away from the steps and seemed to be studying something.

"Oh…hi." She smiled a beautiful little girl-like grin while sheepishly scrunching up her shoulders, hugging tightly the note-book she was carrying. She was dressed in a stylish red and black workout outfit with her hair pulled back in a ponytail. "I was just admiring the beautiful carvings on your front door! What is that? Some sort of…" She struggled to find the right word. A light breeze blew her bangs across her face, so she freed up a hand to hold them back as she waited for Jonathon to respond. He felt himself holding his breath, noticing how pretty she looked with her hair completely away from her face.

"Ya…it's a family crest of sorts…has to do with our British heritage and our last name. Something like that…I actually don't remember the exact details." Jonathon chuckled, trying to ease the awkwardness. He stood staring at the door as if he'd never really taken a good look at it. His nerves weren't going away, making him wish he could turn around and puke in the bushes to get rid of them. *She is really right here at my house*! An abrupt double honk made them both jump and look in the direction of the street. Leana gave her mom a reassuring wave as she drove off. Turning back around, she stood quietly for a few seconds staring at the door, waiting for Jonathon's next move. When he didn't say anything right away, she broke the silence. "She's running an errand. I can text her if we finish before she comes back."

Jonathon realized he was making her wait and apologetically stepped back, pulling the door open further, motioning an invitation. "So…come on in. My notes are upstairs in my room." Out of the corner of his eye, he spotted Lulu poking her head out the kitchen entry wearing a knowing smirk. He quickly turned to walk toward the stairs, hoping Leana would follow and not notice Lulu spying.

"What a nice house, Jon. Thanks again for inviting me to come by. I kinda needed to get away from my place for a while." Leana followed slowly behind Jonathon, looking around. "That's why I met Jasper yesterday. It was just…" she seemed to be choosing her words very carefully. "…nice to get out. So many relatives staying at the house and getting things ready for the funeral."

Jonathon slowed on the steps and turned to look at her as they continued up. He wanted to ask where in the heck JR was on a Friday night but thought it would be rude to change the subject. "Ya. You mentioned that at The Coffee Couch." Jonathon gave her a sympathetic, consoling look before continuing up the stairs. "I was kinda surprised to run into you guys." He was dying to blurt out several questions but refrained. "You don't mind coming up here… to my room, do you? Our housekeeper is here."

"Of course not. I won't stay long. Just want to look at the notes before I leave, in case I need you to clarify something."

They entered Jonathon's room and he pulled out his desk chair to offer her a seat. As he walked past her to go sit on his bed,

Leana commented, "You smell good. I've never noticed that before." She then blushed. "I mean…like in class, when we work together, I haven't noticed you wearing cologne…" One of her hands was flying around in a fluster as she tried to explain. She was clearly embarrassed.

"I don't usually wear it at school." Now, Jonathon was the one feeling embarrassed. He basically just admitted that he put it on today, especially for her. He felt his face heating up yet again, wishing he'd worn a lighter-weight shirt. His mind raced, trying to think of something to say, and feeling absolutely devastated by his stupid attempt to impress her with cologne. Then he and Leana looked at each other and after a brief pause, both started laughing. He then cleared his throat and took a deep breath, thankful for the ice breaker and happy she saw the humor in the situation, too.

"So…" Jonathon started but noticed Leana was distracted and looking around the room with curiosity.

"What's that thing?" Leana was staring at his Machine. Jonathon tried not to panic. It crossed his mind at that moment; if he played his cards right, this "project" might go easier than he had expected.

"That…oh…it's nothing. Well, nothing THAT big a deal. It's just a machine I kinda built to help me relax when I do homework." *A little white lie.* he thought. Leana stood up and walked over to the Machine, running her hand along the top as she assessed it. "That's cool. Does it really work?"

"It works for me. You'll have to try it sometime."

"I can try it out today," Leana quickly interjected, surprising Jonathon. "You can go over the notes with me first and then I'll use the machine, so it'll all soak in." She grinned and looked down at him sitting on the edge of his bed. Her direct eye contact made him feel uneasy. "Or…does it work the other way around? If I use the machine first to relax me and THEN you go over the notes, will they soak in better that way?" Jonathon began to wonder if she was taunting him. *Or is she genuinely curious*?

"Well…it can work either way." He took a gulp as he looked down at the ground and fidgeted with his feet. "Probably makes a difference depending on how you usually prefer to study." He looked back up at her. She was still smiling at him, making him now feel extremely uncomfortable. *Is she flirting?* He'd never had any girl, especially one he liked, show this much interest in him.

Leana went back to the chair to sit down. Jonathon pursed his lips and blew out a slow, deep breath, picking up a pillow to quickly pat his forehead while she wasn't looking. He made a reach for the drawer where he was keeping the envelope holding the notes. As he did, his arm brushed hers and she didn't move away. *This girl is not shy,* he thought. *What would JR think of her sitting here?* Several questions rushed his mind. Jonathon handed the pale green envelope to Leana.

"Whoa. Are these the notes? How formal." She smiled. "I love sage green."

Jonathon thought to take a mental note of this fact. "Is that what you call it? I just thought it was light green." Now he felt stupid making small talk and wished he had found a standard white business envelope.

Leana ran her finger over her name, which Jonathon had taken great care in writing out neatly. "You have really nice writing." He felt his palms beginning to sweat and he wondered how he could possibly concentrate on the chemistry notes.

Leana began digging through her handbag. She took out a pair of white framed designer glasses and put them on before opening the envelope, giving her a smart, sophisticated look. She started reading through the notes as he stared, mesmerized, watching her lips move as if reading out loud but no sound was coming out.

"Here's a question for you." Her words snapped him out of his trance. "This talks about physical properties of matter. There are seven...appearance, texture..." she used her right hand and brushed her left arm lightly, to emphasize "texture". "Odor, such as your cologne." Jonathon rolled his eyes at that and they both chuckled. "And there's melting point and boiling point..." she lifted her eyes to meet Jonathon's with a look that seemed dreamy to him. "Do *people* have melting points and boiling points, Jon?"

Jonathon stood up and fast-tracked it across the room and then paced back. *What was she asking?* He thought he had been nervous before she arrived but now; he suddenly wished she wasn't in his room at all. His entire body felt clammy.

He started to answer but she cut him off and started to laugh. "That was just a hypothetical question, Jon. I was only trying to memorize the seven properties out loud. That didn't quite come out right." She giggled and he felt ridiculous for thinking she was being forward. His body relaxed a little with relief.

Leana turned back to the notes, burying her head into the pages. She was clearly trying to forget about what she had just said. Jonathon sat quietly for a few minutes while she read. Growing impatient, he decided it was now or never. "Would you like to try out the Machine while you're reading?"

"Oh." She set the notes down and twisted around to look at the machine. "Sure…I guess. How does it work?"

"I'll just put these small little conductor patches on your temples here and here." He reached and touched each side of her head to show her. He felt a tingle of excitement rush up his arms at the touch, then took a deep breath. "I need to attach these wires to the patches. You can listen to music through these noise-cancelling headphones." He handed her the headphones and picked up the wires to attach the conductor pads quickly before she changed her mind.

"What do the wires do?" she furrowed her brow, staring at what he was doing.

"It's just a light impulse that helps you retain what you're reading or studying." They activate when you put on the headphones, and I hit the ON button, of course."

Leana paused as she contemplated. "OK. Do I sit here or...?"

"No…No…" he jumped off the bed where he had been sitting and straightened the coverlet, offering her to lie down with a polite hand gesture.

Just as Leana stood to go to the bed, there was a light tap on the door which startled them both. Lulu called out, "Can I bring you some lemonade or cookies, Jon-Jon?"

Jonathon immediately brought a hand to his mouth and squeezed his eyes shut, a reflex to hearing her use his pet name. Leana giggled again. "That's okay, Lulu, thanks," he softly yelled back to the closed door. Not wanting to be rude he then turned to offer Leana a say in the matter. "That is…unless you want some?"

"Oh, no thank you." Leana, yelled back across the door. When no more offers came from Lulu, they heard steps walking away. Leana then sat on the side of the bed. "Shall I take my shoes off?"

"Only if you want to." Jonathon walked over to REMY and uncoiled the wires with the already attached conductor pads. He wheeled the table with his machine toward the bed where Leana was now laying like Sleeping Beauty with her hands folded across her stomach and her eyes closed. "What kind of music do you like?" he asked while getting the headphones set up.

"I love Luke Bryan. And most country if it's not too…twangy." She opened her eyes to peer over toward Jonathon and sensed he didn't know who she was talking about. "Actually, I like most anything. I even like old-fashioned stuff my parents listen to."

"So do I!" He was excited to hear she had a fondness for classics. Suddenly there was another knock on the door. "Yes, Lulu?" He yelled a little louder than last time and threw a frustrated glance toward the door.

"Miss Kate is at the door." Lulu called out. Jonathon grabbed his cellphone to look at the time. It was only 11:00 and he could have sworn they decided on noon.

"OK. Can you tell her I'll be down in a minute?" Frustrated, Jonathon set the headphones and conductor pads back on his Machine and looked over at Leana who was now sitting on the edge of the bed. "You know Kate, don't you? We've been friends forever. She was supposed to come over at noon to interview me about the debate team…for the school paper. I'm not sure why she's here so early but if you wait here…I'm sorry, is that ok? I'll see if she can come back later."

Leana started to get up, but Jonathon motioned for her to stay put as he jetted out of the room, not giving her a choice.

Rushing down the stairs, he briefly looked back over his shoulder to make sure he'd closed his door. The last thing he needed was for Lulu to walk by and see his machine all set up and Leana sitting on the bed.

In the entrance hall, Kate stood in washed out blue jeans, white Converse tennis shoes and a gingham top looking like a picture-perfect girl next door. She took a few steps toward Jonathon as she saw him coming. "I'm sorry I'm early. I hope Leana isn't still here. I have to meet my mom for lunch at 12:30, so I was hoping we could start a little early."

Jonathon put his hands on each of Kate's shoulders and looked at her square in the eyes. "Look, Kate…actually she is still here. Can we do this after your lunch?"

The sound of footsteps made them both turn to notice Leana trotting down the stairs.

Jonathon felt panic setting in. *What was she doing? She can't leave now!*

She rounded the end of the bannister and slowed when she noticed them watching her. "Oh, hi, Kate." Kate simply gave a little wave and Leana looked to Jonathon, nervously holding her hands out with an apologetic look. "Hey, thanks, Jon." She held up the sage envelope in acknowledgement. "My mom just texted she is on her way over. Guess she thought we'd had plenty of time to go over the notes. I'll try the Machine another time." With that, she eased past Kate and slid out the front door.

"Machine?" Kate eyed Jonathon with a questioning look.

"Just stay here a minute!" he demanded as he left Kate standing alone with Lulu lurking down the hall.

Outside, Leana was standing on the sidewalk waiting for her mother. Jonathon jogged out toward her. "Hey…sorry about that. Thanks for coming over."

"Well, it's ME that needs to thank YOU. I appreciate it. Really." She paused and then asked "Um…do you know, well I'm sure you do…but Jasper doesn't have a girlfriend, or anything does he?"

Jonathon felt completely taken aback. The look on his face could have easily given away his true feelings but he quickly recovered and retorted, "Why? You have a boyfriend, don't you?"

"Geez, Jon!" She took a step backwards and gripped her notebook across her chest.

"I was just wondering!" Then she turned her back to Jonathon and glared down the street.

He looked up to the sky with his hands in his pockets and inhaled deeply trying to calm the anger building up inside toward Jasper. Leana quickly turned back around. "Not that it makes any difference, but I think JR and I are breaking up. We talked about it last week and we haven't exactly had much communication this week." She looked down at the ground and Jonathon wasn't sure how or if he should respond. Still staring at the ground, she continued. "I think he just feels sorry for me about my grandfather and doesn't want to make me sadder by flat out labeling it right now." She glanced up to see Jonathon's dazed expression. "Were you thinking I'm a cheater? Is that why you seem mad at me for asking about Jasper?"

Jonathon now felt cornered. What was he to say? That may have crossed his mind along with many other thoughts but he knew there was only one main reason for his reaction. *It's because I really like you,* he wanted to say. *So much that I want to make you dream about me!*

He looked at her standing with a questioning look and wondered what he should do. *Does she like Jasper a little? Or a lot?* He cautiously proceeded. "Look, Leana. I don't think you're a cheater." Her face softened a little at his remark. "And…I don't think Jasper is seeing anyone." White lie again…because he knew for sure Jasper never had a girlfriend or even talked about a female in a fond way until Leana. They stood for a moment in awkward silence, giving Jonathon time to reflect on the entire scenario.

"I was just curious," Leana murmured. A gust of wind came up and she clutched the collar of her workout jacket to protect her neck from the chill as she looked watchfully for her mom's car. "I don't really know what's going on right now, Jon. I'm just glad to have a friend who cares." Jonathon wasn't sure if she was speaking about him or Jasper. He raised his eyebrows much the way Lulu often does when she is questioning things. This spoke loud and clear to Leana. "I mean…two friends. You both are really nice to be here for me this week. I get why you guys are best friends." Jonathon gave an appreciative nod even though it wasn't exactly what he was hoping she'd say.

"Whatever I can do to help out," Jonathon stammered. He was using the toe of his shoe to swipe the crack in the sidewalk back and forth while trying to muster up some courage to ask her a question. Suddenly, he stopped, took a deep breath and looked straight at Leana. "Are you going to the dance next week?"

Leana looked completely stunned. "Uh…I am not sure. I mean…because I was supposed to go with JR but since I'm not sure about what is happening with us…" she trailed off. He sensed her feeling uncomfortable.

Trying to recover and avoid humiliation, Jonathon thought quickly and declared, "I might go but I haven't been to one before, so I was just hoping I'd know a few people there…that's all."

Leana looked embarrassed after hearing his explanation. "Oh." She giggled shyly. "I thought you were asking me to go with you." Just then Leana's mom pulled up to the curb and rolled down her window. Jonathon felt aggravated he screwed up the opportunity to actually ask her to the dance.

"Hi, Mrs. Parker." Jonathon walked around to the other side to open the passenger door for Leana as her mom gave a recognizing smile.

"Hi, Jon. It's so nice of you to help Leana out."

"Oh, no problem!" he answered as Leana slid into the car. Before closing her door, in a quieter tone, he addressed Leana. "So…I guess I'll see you in chemistry on Monday. I hope the funeral goes well." Immediately, he felt stupid, thinking he could have come up with a more appropriate comment about the funeral.

Leana smiled through the closed window and mouthed, "Thanks." They drove away, leaving Jonathon standing in the middle of the street watching their departing taillights. Disappointed, he thought he would now have to figure out another way to get Leana back over to use REMY.

Slowly sauntering back toward the house and thinking about what had happened he suddenly remembered Kate was inside. He had completely forgotten she was there. He sprinted for the door and just as he got to it Lulu heaved it open with her small frame.

"I was just coming to find you. I thought you got lost. I had Miss Kate wait up in your room."

Jonathon's jaw dropped as he shot his eyes up the staircase, noticing his bedroom door closed. *What have I done?* he thought. He dashed up the steps praying Kate had left everything alone.

Jonathon burst into his room, hoping he'd find Kate sitting quietly waiting. She was…only she had the wires on her forehead and the headphones on. She jumped at Jonathon's rushed entrance with a gasp.

"Oh gosh, Jon…you scared me!" She pulled the headphones off, letting them drape around her neck like a scarf.

Jonathon stood with his mouth gaping, unable to respond.

"Jon? You okay?" Kate sat looking bewildered at her longtime friend and then reached up to snap her fingers in front of his face.

Jonathon's mind was whirling with dread, thinking about what had just happened. *Has she just activated REMY?* He slowly emerged from his trance and stood staring at Kate. The two conductors attached to each side of her forehead were hanging like wilted antennas. They were meant to be placed on the temple area, but he doubted it would make a huge difference in their ability to transmit his programmed dream…the one intended for Leana.

Jonathon took a step toward Kate in a resigned slump and gently pulled the two conductors from her face. "Sorry to keep you waiting," he slowly muttered as he laid them across the top of REMY and put a hand out, silently asking for her to hand over the headphones.

Kate sat still using only her eyes to follow him as he walked over to his desk chair and plopped down in a look of defeat. She gulped and folded her arms across her chest in a protective manner. "Did I…do something wrong?"

Jonathon had his arms resting on his desk now and was holding his head in his hands. What seemed like forever to Kate was only about 10 seconds before he finally spoke. "I suppose you still need this interview. But I am kinda tired."

"You're tired? Babysitting knocked it out of me!" Kate swung her head back in a dramatic display of exasperation until she realized Jonathon was ignoring her. She leaned forward and cautiously asked, "Are you sick or something?"

After another moment of awkward silence, Jonathon sat up straight to face Kate. "OK…shoot. Let's make this quick." He then laid back and stretched his arms out and clasped his hands behind his head. His mind was spinning. *Jasper now apparently has the hots for Leana. Leana may now have a thing for Jasper. And now…Leana thinks I am accusing her of cheating on JR. And, if REMY had time to make an impression on Kate, she could start dreaming about me this very evening! What else could go wrong?!* He made a frustrated "Hmmpf" sound, but then realized Kate had said something.

"You didn't even hear my first question," Kate frowned as she stared at Jonathon who seemed to be coming out of a trance. "But I have an entirely different question instead. This caught Jonathon's attention. "Are you mad at me?" She turned and pointed at REMY. "And…what IS this machine? I only heard music." With that, Jonathon sat up straight again and dropped his jaw, making Kate suddenly feel the need to apologize for being nosy. "Sorry, I was just bored sitting here."

Jonathon fell back into the chair. "That's two questions," he quipped mockingly. Though he was half-joking, when he noticed Kate's defensive change of expression, he quickly added. "It's really nothing, Kate." He stared back at the cute fading freckles left over from her youth, now crinkling up on her nose as she frowned. "The machine is…" he cringed at the lie he was about to tell, especially when she sat wearing a vulnerable, trusting look while waiting for his explanation. Still, he felt he had no choice. He couldn't confess what he was up to. "It's an experiment to help me relax during my studies." He hoped this would be enough for her to ease up on her inquiry and get to the interview.

Apparently not satisfied, Kate started to ask more. "But what are the…" A loud knock broke up her question and they both turned, expecting the door to open.

"Jon-Jon? Do you and Kate want some lemonade now?" Lulu hollered.

Jonathon felt that for once, her knocks couldn't have come at a better time. He smiled at Kate. "Sure, Lulu…and we'll take some cookies, too." He heard her hurried footsteps transcending the stairs.

"Can we get started? Don't you have to meet your mom for lunch in a little bit?" Jonathon asked. He felt thankful when Kate seemed to have forgotten she was in the middle of a question before Lulu's interruption. She opened her phone and deployed the app that would record her interview about his debate team. Jonathon did his best to stay focused as he watched his light-hearted friend of 10 years spiel off question after question.

Throughout the interview, Jonathon pondered several possibilities with concern. *What is this going to lead to if she starts dreaming about me? Will our friendship end? Could it really change Kate's feelings toward me?* In between answering her questions, he studied her face while reflecting on his current problem. *I need to fix this as soon as possible...but how?*

No longer than a half hour and a small plate of cookies later, Kate closed the phone app and her notebook after jotting down a last note. Looking across the room, she wondered why Jonathon's mind seemed somewhere on another planet. Although he answered all of her questions, she knew him well enough to know he was distracted.

"What are you doing tonight? You and Jasper hanging out?" Kate probed, oblivious to recent developments between him and Jasper.

Jonathon paused, rousing at the mention of Jasper's name. "We don't have plans...but I need to talk with him, so maybe."

Kate waited a moment. When it didn't appear she was going to get an invite to join the guys, she lied. "I should do homework tonight." Jonathon just sat shaking his head in acknowledgement, so Kate stood to go.

"Tessa is hanging out with Bryan Corwin…going bowling with a bunch of kids."

Jonathon flinched with surprise at this bit of gossip. "Realllly?" he chuckled. "Why aren't you going?"

Kate had lied about having homework, but she really didn't want to go bowling with a bunch of kids who were coupled up. "I'd go if you were going." When she noticed Jonathon's immediate tongue-tied reaction, she quickly jumped to give him an out. "But like I said…homework," and gave a quirky half-smile, shrugging her shoulders.

"Look…" Jonathon said as he also stood to open the door. "I'm sorry. I'm in a weird mood today."

Kate studied his face. "That's fine," she reluctantly offered. "Maybe I'll see you in church tomorrow."

A soft floral fragrance lingered behind Kate as Jonathon followed her down the stairs to the front door and he suddenly remembered the cologne he was wearing to impress Leana. Feeling a little embarrassed, he wondered if Kate had noticed, but glad she never brought it up.

When they got to the door, Kate turned to say goodbye. "Hope you guys have more fun than I do tonight." She winked and shut the door behind her. Jonathon felt a knot in his stomach, wondering what dream she might have that night.

The whole debacle left Jonathon feeling mentally exhausted, so he rushed back upstairs to take a nap. Before laying his head down, he erased the dream he'd inputted for Leana, then programmed a simple dream of him lounging on a floating mattress up at the nearby lake, something he felt would take his mind off his misguided project. Barely remembering his head hitting the pillow or connecting himself to REMY, he awoke nearly three hours later to the sound of a distant lawnmower.

Lying with his eyes closed and letting his mind wander, he suddenly panicked, bolting up as he began to recall a dream he just had during his nap. *Why was Kate in my dream?* The dream he programmed did not include any information about her. He sat confused for a moment but then realized he must have only dreamed about her because of their recent encounter. He threw his head back on his pillow for a few minutes longer. "Kate, Kate, Kate," he whispered to himself. *What on earth is going to happen next?* he wondered.

Jonathon took a cold washcloth to his face and then tried to wipe off any remnant of cologne before heading downstairs. Through the walls, he could hear his parents arguing down the hall, causing him to worry a little. Of course, kids aren't usually privy to information about their parents' private matters, but it seemed to Jonathon, that they never used to fight. Now it was a regular occurrence.

When their voices stopped, and he heard footsteps going down the stairs, Jonathon decided to give them some space. He opened his phone and caught up on social media postings and answered an e-mail chain between his debate teammates. He then researched some information for his debate club that needed to be done by Monday. When he finished, he sat thinking for a moment, took a deep sigh and decided to text Jasper.

We need to talk. You busy?

In less than a minute he got a reply.

Busy tonight. Talk to u tomorrow

Seriously??!! Busy the entire night? Jonathon's irritation stretched his wandering mind to its limits. *Is he going out with Leana on a real date this time?* He couldn't believe this! He looked at his phone. It was 4:40 p.m. He bolted down the stairs where only his mom was seated having a cup of tea. Lulu was elbow high in baking flour at the counter.

"Mom…mind if I use the car for just a little…like an hour or two?"

His mom's eyes looked puffy, and he wondered if she had been crying. She kept her eyes low and acted like she had something she was trying to get out of her eye with her pinky finger.

"I'm sorry, honey. Your dad has his car and I promised Lulu she could take mine for an outing since I'm staying in. Where do you need to go, maybe she can give you a ride?"

Lulu looked up with an astonished look before quickly turning her head back to what she was doing. "Nothing important," Jonathon answered. "I'm just going to go for a little walk then. I'll see you later." He started to leave the kitchen but then turned around. "Where's dad?"

"He..." Jonathon sensed a slight hesitation from his mother. "…he just went out for a little while. He is meeting a client."

Sensing his mother's discomfort at what might possibly be a lie, Jonathon just gave her a grin and a nod as he turned again to leave. "I might just grab a bite while I'm out so, don't count on me for dinner." Then, he walked back over to give his mom a kiss on the top of her head. He felt she needed it. She reached up and gave him a hug with one arm in a thankful gesture.

Walking down his street past the neatly manicured yards with groomed hedges and nicely mown lawns, Jonathon took in the calming essence of his neighborhood. Many matured trees scattered the landscape and he inhaled deeply to take in the smell of the eucalyptus trees lining the road. After walking about five blocks, he rounded a corner to head toward their small town's main drag. Downtown was a different direction from his home than Cascadia High but about an equal walking distance. Coming upon an area of several small businesses and shops, the town seemed to be just getting started on this Saturday afternoon, as workers from restaurants with outdoor seating were setting up tables.

Passing one of the newest wine-tasting venues, Jonathon spotted a couple sitting at a high-top table in a fenced-off outdoor area. He recognized them as a couple he'd met at an event with his parents. Flipping them a wave of his hand, he hurried past. He wasn't in the mood to stop and chat.

As he continued to stroll the sidewalk, he noticed his old friend Sol and a few of Sol's buddies up ahead sitting on a curb with their skateboards, chatting. He crossed the street to avoid them, but Sol turned just then, catching Jonathon's eye. Jonathon felt compelled to wave but kept walking, acting like he was in a hurry to get somewhere. A sudden gust of wind whipped through the street, and he found himself wishing he had thrown on a light jacket. To shake off the chill, he ducked into The Coffee Couch for something warm to drink.

Inside was bustling but Jonathon didn't see anyone he knew well, only a few acquaintances. After getting his order, he went to stand by a large bay window viewing the street. He leaned against a pillar, one hand in his jean's pocket. Using his free hand to sip his mocha, steam wafted up, fogging his glasses. He was about to venture outdoors again when out of the corner of his eye he thought he noticed Jasper's yellow, slightly beat-up Mustang parked on the street one door down. He removed his glasses and cleaned them with a napkin he found lying on a nearby table. When he put his glasses back on and confirmed it to be Jasper's car, Jonathon looked again around The Coffee Couch to make sure Jasper wasn't there. He wondered if he might find him next door in the bookstore or less likely, in the hardware store two doors down.

He waited for a few customers to make their way inside before slipping through the exit door and out onto the sidewalk. Surveying the area, he saw no sign of Jasper. While trying to decide if he should go looking or just wait until Jasper returned to his car, Jonathon felt dread about confronting his friend. Before he had time to make a decision, Jasper's voice caught him off guard and Jonathon spun around.

"Hey, Jon." Jasper was standing next to him, fidgeting nervously. "I saw you as you were walking in, so I stopped to maybe catch ya for a few." Jasper was sporting a new army-green jacket and tan jeans, a little dressier look than his usual. He stood, swaying with a concerned look on his face waiting for Jonathon's response. "I have about 20 minutes."

Jonathon remembered Jasper saying he was busy this evening, so he knew he'd better use this time to clear up some things while he had a chance. "Let's go see if we can find a table inside." Jasper nodded and followed as Jonathon led the way. They found a small booth toward the back, just being cleared by the barista.

After they sat, Jasper picked up the menu on the table for about 10 seconds before tossing it back down and getting up to go place an order. "Back in a minute."

Jonathon rehearsed what he wanted to say while he was waiting for his friend to return. When Jasper came back with his coffee, he slid in and leaned forward as if he was about to say something to Jonathon but then sat there with a dumbfounded look on his face. "Yes?" Jonathon groaned sarcastically.

Jasper leaned back a little. He smacked his lips with a nervous energy before speaking. "Your Machine works great, just so you know. I may have listened a little… with those headphones." He was rushing his sentences, barely taking a breath. When Jonathon maintained a seething gaze, Jasper was quick to defend himself. "Well, *you* left that drawing right out on your desk, so it was easy to figure out…" He lowered his eyes. "I'm having dreams about her now, every time I sleep, even if it's a 10-minute nap! Even when I'm not sleeping! I can't help myself!" He then slouched back in the booth staring at Jonathon, looking exhausted as if he'd just run a marathon.

Jonathon didn't have to ask who Jasper was talking about. He sat staring at a face he knew so well and that he cared about. His friend looked smitten. Several seconds passed before Jonathon very quietly answered. "I don't blame you. I just wish you would have let me be the one to hook you up to use the machine instead of sneaking into my room…and intercepting the wrong dream."

"I didn't sneak into your room! When have I ever needed to sneak into your room…or your house?" Jasper's energy reignited.

"Sorry…I don't mean it like that. It's just…I was TRYING to get you to come over. If you hadn't come in and helped yourself to REMY, this wouldn't have happened. It was programed for a Leana dream because I had been using it for myself. I would have programmed it about *any* other girl in the entire school…or anything else you wanted if I knew you would finally give it a try!" Jonathon felt frustration at something that was now too late to fix.

"REMY?" Jasper frowned in question but chuckled at the name.

"It's just a name I gave my Machine, so I don't have to call it 'my Machine' when I'm talking about it…to you, since you're the only friend that really knows why I built it." Jonathon had lowered his voice to a harsh whisper and looked around to view if anyone else was listening. Jasper had a puzzled look on his face, so Jonathon continued. "You know…REM, for rapid eye movement. REMY. I haven't even had a chance to tell you." Jasper gave a wry smile as Jonathon started to feel his patience waning. "Who cares now anyway? This isn't about a name."

Jasper let the whole rundown soak in. "So, are you really dreaming about her all of the time too?" Jasper queried.

"What do you think?" Jonathon blurted out in a yell. He looked around again, then hushed his voice. "I am the one that built the thing all because of her!" Jasper sat silently looking around the coffee shop, everywhere except straight at Jonathon. Jonathon leaned back in the booth, thinking. *He seems like he's dreaming about her more than I do!*

While the two of them sat drinking their drinks in an awkward silence, Jonathon glanced out the window and saw Kate standing over by one of the parking meters talking to a very tall guy with a hoodie on. At least he looked to be tall, standing next to his petite friend. He straightened up to focus on the window, which made Jasper turn around to look also.

"What are you looking at?" Jasper asked.

Jonathon wished the guy would turn around. Kate seemed quite happy and was clutching the meter like a carousel pole, swinging back and forth, and laughing. "Kate's outside. She is talking to someone."

Jasper partially stood to get a better look. "So..." He sat back down.

Jonathon relaxed back into the seat but kept a watchful eye out the window, pretending he didn't care either, though his curiosity was killing him.

"Anyway…I want to take Leana on a date…" Jasper blurted out. "…if she says yes."

"Of course, you do!" Jonathon shot back in a sarcastic drawl.

"You know…she and JR broke up," stated Jasper.

"News travels fast." Jonathon couldn't resist being sarcastic. "Actually, I heard it wasn't officially a breakup yet." Just then the towering guy with a hoodie turned toward the window and was looking in their direction. Jonathon wasn't sure if the guy was able to see inside through the reflective glass. Jonathon whipped his head back around toward Jasper.

"It's JR."

"Huh?" Jasper turned again toward the window but then turned back around and gave off a short little laugh. "Like I said…so?" Noticing Jonathon's clenched jaw and unsettled demeanor, he softened. "I don't like us not getting along. I don't know how to change how I feel. I could get you to hook me up to the machine again to dream about someone else but…"

Jonathon scowled. "But what?"

"I don't really want to stop liking her, if I'm being honest."

Jonathon looked out the window again and the two were gone. He stood to try to get a better view. When he couldn't see Kate or JR, he dropped back down and squeezed his eyes shut, reaching up to rub them as if he had a splitting headache. He took a deep breath before speaking again. "I don't know. I need to think about this. Did you know Kate was friends with JR?"

Jasper gave Jonathon a puzzled look. "Who cares?"

Jonathon began wringing his hands, occasionally glancing out the window. "I don't care. Just seems odd, you know?"

Jasper chuckled. "Whatever, dude. I gotta go." With that he stood up and smiled.

"It'll all work out how it's supposed to." He did his classic knuckle punch lightly into Jonathon's shoulder and left Jonathon simply sitting there staring at the wall ahead, feeling defeated.

A few minutes later, he decided to order another strong coffee before going outside to get some fresh air. He felt bothered by Kate keeping company with JR but wasn't sure why. Maybe he just felt dislike for JR because he had been Leana's boyfriend. For all he knew, he was probably a pretty nice guy. And, after all, Jonathon hadn't offered to hang out with Kate tonight when she had asked what he was doing.

He left The Coffee Couch, scanning the street for JR who would be easier to spot in a crowd than Kate. There was no sign of either of them, so he began walking back toward the school. Just as he was crossing the street, he noticed Jasper's yellow car at a stop sign up ahead. He watched it make the turn and spotted who he thought to be Leana in the passenger seat. *What a jerk!* he thought. *Nice of him to tell me he wanted to take her out when he had it planned all along!* It was getting a little colder outside but his blood was boiling, so he barely noticed.

He diverted the direct route to the school and decided to swing into Grocer's Corner to grab something for dinner from the deli inside. They had a few seats in a sectioned off area just outside for patrons to sit down to eat. Jonathon sat down at a table waiting for his order and flagged down an employee to turn on the outdoor heater next to him. He was eating his sandwich and a bag of chips, trying to forget about everything for the time being, when he noticed his mom's car pulling into the parking lot. Lulu's head could barely be seen behind the large steering wheel, which Jonathon found comical as he watched from a distance. She backed into a spot toward one end of the lot, so she was now facing the store. The headlights went out, but Lulu remained inside, slouching down low.

Jonathon continued to munch down his dinner while keeping an eye on Lulu. *What is she doing?* he wondered. When he finished eating, he decided to stay seated to observe Lulu, wondering what she was up to. He knew she wouldn't ask to borrow the car just to come sit in a parking lot. Jonathon scrolled through his phone while he waited, frequently looking up so he wouldn't miss anything. After about 15 minutes without any activity, he was getting bored. He got up to throw his wrappers in the trash when he saw her getting out of the car. She was in a dress and had her hair down but pulled back with two barrettes, something he seldom saw at home. She seemed to be in a hurry to get across the lot to the store entrance, when suddenly he noticed Mr. Mercado approaching the store's automated sliding doors from a different direction. Mr. Mercado was about to grab a cart when Lulu who had grabbed a cart from the lot came barreling his way, almost colliding with Jonathon's teacher. Then Lulu seemed to be acting apologetic. Jonathon couldn't believe what he was witnessing! *She must have figured out when Mr. Mercado does his shopping and now is deliberately running into him so she could talk to him!*

Jonathon sat back down and leaned forward rubbing his head in his hands to hide his face and prevent the two from noticing him watching. He continued to peek between his fingers and wondered what on earth Lulu could be saying to engage Mr. Mercado for better than five minutes. Jonathon noticed her jovial mannerisms, almost...flirty. *Has my Machine really done such a number on her that she is taking desperate measures to meet him?* While watching, Jonathon wondered if Mr. Mercado was married, realizing he'd never had reason to think about it before now.

He observed Mr. Mercado offering Lulu to go into the store ahead of him. As she did, his teacher followed. Jonathon had to hand it to her, she must have been patiently plotting this meeting. How Lulu was reacting to a dream or dreams was exactly what Jonathon had wanted from Leana. He had wanted her to think about him. To pursue him.

But now he felt he had screwed it all up.

Contemplating going inside to watch Lulu stalk her victim, he decided to just head home instead. He felt exhausted thinking about everything and in the 10-minute brisk walk home, he came up with another Leana dream to program that night.

When Jonathon walked in the door, he found his mother sitting alone on the couch watching the news. She started to get up but then sat back down when she discovered it was Jonathon. "Oh, hello, honey. I thought it was your father…" her voice trailed off sounding disappointed.

"Is everything okay, mom?" He decided it couldn't hurt to just ask.

"Of course, honey. Everything is fine." Jonathon noticed a forced smile and a small furrow in her brow as she answered. "Do you want anything to eat? I think there's some soup in the fridge that Lulu made earlier."

Though he doubted his mom's sincerity at the moment, he couldn't imagine discussing personal matters about his dad with her. Still, he wished he could help. "I had a sandwich in town but thanks. I am super tired. Think I'll just go on up and hang out in my room and do some homework." He went over, and like earlier, gave his mother another kiss on her forehead and whispered, "Good night."

The next morning, Jonathon woke up feeling slightly anxious by his latest dream. It was similar to what he had programmed… only Kate and J.R. were also in the dream. He had input a dream about Leana coming over to his house, using REMY and telling Jonathon she didn't like Jasper. However, in the dream he just had, Leana was hooked up to REMY while Kate and JR were also in the room. Kate was sitting on JR's lap watching with curiosity. JR had his one arm around Kate's waist and was trying to pull the cords out of the Machine with the other hand. Jonathon awoke in the middle of the dream when he was trying to block JR from sabotaging the whole process.

It seemed so real. He bolted up in bed, trying to shake off his aggravation. It wasn't quite the dream he had planned to enjoy. Kicking off his covers and flinging his feet to the floor, he quickly threw on a pair of flannel pajama bottoms and headed to the kitchen.

Lulu was already deep into the makings of a hearty Sunday morning breakfast when Jonathon walked in. She glanced at Jonathon, looking like she had just won the lottery.

"Good Sunday morning, Jon-Jon!" she beamed.

He couldn't help but smirk a little, knowing (at least partly) why she was so happy.

"Good morning, Lulu. How is Mr. Mercado?"

Lulu swung around with her mouth hanging wide open. Then she looked over her shoulder toward the door, making sure no one was around, clearly stunned by his question. "What…I mean how…I mean…what do you mean?"

Jonathon walked over to the kitchen sink where Lulu stood. With a look resembling panic, she did not take her eyes off him. Once they were face to face, Jonathon leaned over and used a hushed voice in case his parents were somewhere close by. "I saw you last night…at the grocery store."

Lulu's eyes widened and she began biting her lower lip. Grabbing hold of Jonathon's arm, she babbled a confession. "I can't help it!" she whispered in a desperate tone. "I…" She stopped and looked down.

"It's okay, Lulu. I know you used my Machine. I'm not sure how you hooked it up but you've been dreaming about Mr. Mercado. Am I right?"

"YES!" Lulu looked back up with a look of shock. "I'm sorry, Jon-Jon. I never meant to rummage around or do anything. I was just curious." She looked back down. "I only heard music…so I just relaxed for a little bit to listen. But then I started to get all of these weird visions of a man I'd never met…and ever since then…" She stopped when she heard footsteps.

Jonathon's dad came sauntering into the kitchen with his morning paper and sat down at the table. Lulu dropped her grasp and gave another glance up at Jonathon, pleading with her eyes for him to keep this to himself, and then turned around to finish making breakfast.

"Good morning," his dad said blandly as he was opening the morning newspaper.

"Good morning, dad. Where's mom?" Jonathon was surprised his mother wasn't already down. He walked over and had a seat across from his father.

"She's getting ready for church. You ought to go with her, Jon. I'm golfing this morning. She'd like it if you went." Lulu walked over to the table with a cup of coffee for the two of them.

Jonathon suddenly felt perturbed with his father. It seemed he hardly ever did things with the family anymore. Although his dad had never been as committed as his mom to going to church, Jonathon thought it must be months since he accompanied them.

"I think I will." Jonathon looked up at the kitchen clock to figure out how much time he had to get ready. Although Lulu was cooking away and banging around utensils, the room was noticeably void of conversation and Jonathon wished he had brought his phone down with him, so he could browse the internet. He grabbed a small section of the newspaper from the stack his father had set down, though he wasn't really interested in reading at the moment. Soon, Lulu was delivering a beautiful spinach and sausage frittata to the table with a stack of buttered toast.

Jonathon was almost done inhaling the delicious meal when his mother walked into the kitchen dressed in a springy floral skirt with a casual muslin buttoned up top. "You look nice, mom." He complimented her, noticing his dad didn't even look up from his paper. He sensed his mom was also aware of her husband's inattentiveness.

"Why thank you, Jon. Are you coming to church this morning?"

"Ya. I'll go with you. Is Pastor James back from wherever he went with his family? Kenya?" As he asked the question, he realized it had been at least a few weeks since he'd attended service.

His mother gave a baby clap that her son was going to join her. "Yes, yes. They got back two weeks ago. His stories last week were quite interesting. Maybe he'll mention more about their travels today."

Jonathon then excused himself to go upstairs to shower and get ready. He was almost finished getting dressed when there was a knock on his door. It was Lulu. Jonathon offered for her to enter, so she slithered in and quietly shut the door behind her. She turned to him. "So…I can't quit thinking about him. Is it this machine?! Where did you get all of those ideas to put into that thing?" She flayed one hand out like a game show host toward her Jonathon's contraption. Jonathon thought Lulu sounded like a recording of what Jasper had been saying.

"All of those movies you made me watch, Lulu." It was true. Lulu loved watching classic romance movies and often had them on as he grew up, when she thought her little Jon-Jon was busy with a puzzle or drawing. "It might be the Machine." Jonathon now felt guilty as he stared at Lulu's forlorn expression. "You probably received the subliminal dream messaging I had programed as a joke on Jasper." She looked confused so he continued. "I programmed it, so Jasper would dream about Mr. Mercado. Only…I guess you took the liberty of putting on the headphones the day you weren't supposed to be cleaning my room?" Jonathon raised his eyebrows in question. Lulu again nodded slowly, biting her lip with a contrite look. "And Jasper ended up hooking himself up to the Machine the next day when he came up to my room when I wasn't home. I had inputted a dream meant for me. Now he's dreaming about Leana!"

Lulu put her hand over her mouth, flabbergasted.

Jonathon leaned over and put his arm around Lulu to give her a half hug. "Ya…so I don't really know why only one time triggered you to keep dreaming about Mr. Mercado but I kind of suspected this was the case when you acted so weird at the grocery store."

Lulu giggled but then stopped to take a more serious tone. "I think you should make a dream for your dad to dream about your mom."

Jonathon stepped back and looked down at Lulu. "So, it's not my imagination, is it? Dad seems so…disinterested lately. And I've heard them arguing."

Lulu, now solemn, leaned in to whisper. "He needs a kick in the pants if you ask me. The missus tries hard to get him to notice her like in the old days but he would rather keep his nose in the newspaper than talk to his wife! And he has way too many hobbies that don't include her…like golfing and hanging out with his hoity-toity friends." Lulu then recoiled with a look of regret for having said too much about business that wasn't hers.

Jonathon brought his hand to his mouth to play with his lower lip as he let his mind wander for a moment, recalling all of the times his dad wasn't joining the family with activities in the past year. "That wouldn't be a bad idea, Lulu."

"What?" She seemed to have quickly forgotten what she suggested and wasn't following his thought process.

"Getting my dad to use the Machine." Jonathon tilted his head in its direction. "I named it REMY by the way." Lulu still looked confused, but he decided not to explain.

"Maybe we can get him to start dreaming about mom again." Jonathon gave a wink to Lulu. "But..." he was thinking out loud. "How on Earth would we get him to use REMY?"

"I can help!" Lulu was quick to offer without any forethought.

"What do you suggest?" he asked.

"I don't know. Let me think about it and I will let you know. In the meantime, don't worry about me. I am liking my dreams, Jon-Jon." She gave a mischievous smile and Jonathon felt almost embarrassed to imagine what her dreams were about.

"Okay, Lulu. You're on assignment. You figure out a way and I'll program REMY."

Lulu started to slip out the door when she poked her head back in and gave a thumbs-up. "I like the name even though I've never heard a name like that." She nodded toward his machine. "So, what are you gonna do about Jasper?"

THAT...is the question of the day, he thought.

Later, Jonathon and his mom talked Lulu into accompanying them to church. She always went with them on special occasions, but being a Catholic, she preferred mass to their community Christian church service. It was a crisp, spring day with sporadic clouds dotted against the deep blue sky. Jonathon felt refreshed whenever he attended church and was hoping that today he could wipe away last week's saga from his mind, if only for a few hours. His mother had hurried inside to meet some of her friends. A few parishioners were mingling out in front waiting until the last minute to go inside for the service.

Jonathon stood looking up at the cumulus cloud formations.

Lulu came around the corner from the parking lot and walked up to Jonathon before going inside. "What are you thinking about Jon-Jon?"

"You know...these types of clouds can grow and become thunderheads," he stated as a matter of fact.

Lulu lifted her head to observe the large puffy shapes scattered across the sky. She raised her eyebrows at Jonathon in her Lulu fashion. "Thanks for the lesson on clouds, Jon-Jon. I thought you were looking to the heavens for Jesus!"

He chuckled and started walking toward the giant heavily carved entrance doors of the chapel. "You know, these clouds are kinda like my week, Lulu. Start out as something potentially beautiful but...POOF! Turns into a storm." Jonathon shrugged his shoulders and grinned as he held the door open for her.

As she walked past him, she stopped and looked up to Jonathon with a serious look. "But you know Jon-Jon...there is always a rainbow after the storm." With that, she returned a giant grin and patted his hand before slipping inside.

The choir was facing the body of the church from the chancel. Everyone was standing and singing along to the hymns. Jonathon usually tried to find someone he knew to sit with, but the late morning service was packed and had very few spots open except for the very front and back rows. He slid into the pew next to Lulu. As he did, he met Kate's eyes who was seated across the aisle up a few rows. She was looking back at Jonathon with a sweet smile and gave a quick wave. *Did she have the dream I intended for Leana?* The possibility was unnerving for some reason, and he felt himself blush at the thought. Throughout the service, Kate turned to glance over her shoulder toward Jonathon several times. *Is it my imagination that she is looking at me more than usual?*

As the service let out, Jonathon made a quick exit. Kate came running out, reaching him on the lawn under a giant olive tree. She was beaming, making Jonathon wonder even more about her thoughts.

"I got a job at Juniper Books!" she gushed. Jonathon felt a little relief when her excitement wasn't about what he had suspected. *Did she even dream about me, after all?*

"Wow. That's..." Jonathon started to congratulate her, but she interrupted.

"JR's family...well, his aunt, owns the bookstore. Do you know JR? He plays baseball...tall, cute..."

"Ya, I know who he is." He felt irritated at the mention of JR and didn't particularly want to hear a list of his quality characteristics.

"I thought you probably did. Anyway, I have Woodshop with him, and he told me that his aunt was..."

"Wait!" Jonathon interrupted. You take Woodshop?" He gave her a puzzled look.

"I know I told you. Well, maybe I didn't. I switched out of Art at the end of the semester." When she noticed Jonathon's baffled look, she quickly continued. "So he told me his aunt needed him to fill in because someone quit unexpectedly. I think it was that nerdy girl on your debate team…Susan Shooflee." Jonathon nodded an acknowledgement. "Anyway, I told him I needed to get a job, something other than babysitting, so he told his aunt about me. Wasn't that nice of him?"

Jonathon leaned against the tree and took in a deep breath, letting the breeze refresh his senses as he thought for a moment. "I saw you out on the street with him last night. Guess he took you to the store to introduce you?"

"Where were you?" Kate squinted and shielded her eyes as the sun came out from behind a cloud. She was looking up at Jonathon and he noticed her hazel eyes looked golden at that moment. He'd never really paid close attention to details in her face, but the bright daylight was highlighting all her features as she sat waiting for him to answer.

"I was in The Coffee Couch. I was talking to Jasper but then he left, and I was finishing my coffee drink." Jonathon was looking over Kate's shoulder now, having spotted Lulu sitting on the concrete partition next to the church porch with her eyes closed and face held upward toward the sky. "I'll be right there, Lulu," he hollered. Lulu lowered her head and formed a visor with her hands, looking his way. Then she nodded and resumed her prior position.

"Thought you'd be happy for me. About my job." Kate's mouth gave a little pout as she watched his face for a reaction.

"Hey." Jonathon felt bad for not yet offering a congratulations and leaned forward with open arms to give Kate a hug. "I am. Sorry. Of course, I'm happy for you." He rested his chin on the top of her head as she hugged him back. Lulu was now watching the two of them instead of soaking in the sun's rays. He let go of Kate and straightened, taking a step back when he noticed her eyes on them.

"I guess I should go. When do you start your job?" he asked as they began walking towards Lulu.

"I don't know yet. She asked me for one weekday evening and at least one weekend day. She's supposed to call." As they approached Lulu, Kate slowed her pace and seemed hesitant to speak. She then leaned toward Jonathon and lowered her voice to ask him a question. "Did you know JR and Leana broke up?"

Jonathon stopped and turned to face her. He felt her question was out of the blue. To his knowledge, Kate was unaware of his feelings for Leana. "Um…ya. When Leana came by for the chemistry notes she mentioned it, although it seemed like she didn't exactly know what is happening between them."

Kate nodded, then called out to Lulu who was now heading to the car. "Hi, Lulu. How are you?"

Lulu turned around to answer. "Hello, Miss Kate. I'm fine. It is nice to see you."

Kate gave a warm smile, but when Lulu proceeded to the parking lot, Kate slowed, trying to create some space between them. Once Lulu was out of earshot range, she turned to Jonathon, using a soft, sweet voice. "I had a dream about you last night!" Her face flushed and she seemed uncomfortable. Then she started giggling. "I…I can't really tell you about it."

A*ha,* thought Jonathon. *It really did work like I thought it would.* "Why? You don't remember it?" he pressed.

"Oh…I remember it very well. It was just so..." Kate looked around as if making sure no one was close by to hear. "…so…fun, but weird!"

"Weird?" Jonathon wasn't expecting that description.

"Ya…you know, because it was kind of…" She stopped her explanation. "Never mind. It's hot out here in the sun. I need to go type up our interview from yesterday for the paper." She twisted her mouth in a crooked grin and gave a little wave before running off.

Out in the parking lot, Jonathon's mom was standing with a group of ladies in front of their car. Lulu was sitting in the back seat with the door wide open. When Jonathon approached, they all said quick hellos and made small talk for a few minutes before dispersing to their own vehicles.

The short ride home was very quiet. Jonathon, in the passenger seat, looked across the car at his mother as she was driving. Her brow was furrowed even though she wore sunglasses, and her mouth was drawn tight.

"Are you okay, mom?" he asked, deciding he couldn't keep wondering.

She quickly turned to Jonathon, her jaw slightly dropping in surprise. Then she lifted her chin and quickly looked in her rearview mirror to view Lulu before turning her eyes back to the road. Jonathon also looked back at Lulu who was staring out the side window, acting as if she wasn't listening.

"Yes. Of course, honey." His mom leaned over and patted his knee. "I just have a lot on my mind. What are you doing the rest of the day?"

Jonathon noticed his mother had quickly changed the subject, letting him know she didn't want to talk about whatever "things" were on her mind. "Just homework probably." Jonathon again glanced to the backseat and met Lulu's eyes. *Of course, she is listening,* he thought. Right then he made a decision to spend part of the afternoon plotting a way for his dad to use REMY. He needed to help his mom, and he needed Lulu's help to pull it off.

As they approached their two-story brick house and pulled in, Jonathon noticed his father's car in the driveway. "Dad's home kinda early from golf," he remarked.

"Hmm," was the only reply from his mom. She got out of the car and walked around to the side entrance. Jonathon and Lulu met on the walkway toward the front door. Before entering, Lulu tugged on Jonathon's sleeve to get his attention.

"I have an idea, Jon-Jon. Can you bring REMY downstairs or is it too much work?"

Jonathon considered her request for a moment. "I suppose so, Lulu. What are you thinking?"

"I overheard your mom telling one of her friends that she'd meet her this afternoon at that new Tea House over by the river. If your dad is still home, we can get him to come to his study and you can make up some excuse for him to listen to some music or something."

Jonathon was thinking for a moment when the front door flew open. His mother looked bothered. "Jonathon! Can you come help me? Your father has wrenched his back!"

Jonathon and Lulu rushed in behind her and saw his dad painfully stooped by the kitchen door, holding his lower back with one hand, and gripping the door frame with the other. "Can you help me get him over to the couch, Jonathon? Lulu…maybe grab the heating pad. I think it's by my side of our bed." His mom calmly gave out orders as Jonathon attempted to help his dad shuffle to the living room but every time he tried to hold him or help him move, his dad let out a loud groan.

"I need something for the pain!" his dad grumbled as he limped across the room. Slowly, he tried easing onto the couch. Jonathon helped lift his dad's legs one at a time as his mom rushed into the kitchen. She came back with a few pills in her hand and a small glass of water.

"Have you eaten, Jon? You shouldn't take these on an empty stomach." Jonathon rarely heard his mom call his dad by his first name. Usually, it was sweetheart or darling. His father didn't answer and instead let out another moan as he reached for the glass and the pills.

"Here you go, Mr. Samuels," Lulu called out as she jogged back into the living room with the heating pad. She plugged it in next to the nearby lamp and asked him to roll over slightly, so she could shove it under his back. His father moaned even louder as he attempted to turn.

"Thank you, Lulu, all of you. I'll be fine. All I did was swing the club on an approach shot and…" He clinched both fists, indicating the moment his back went out. Mrs. Samuels was standing flat-faced with her arms folded across her waist.

"Well, I guess that's it for golf for a while." Jonathon noticed a hint of sarcasm in his mom's voice. His dad didn't even look up.

"Sorry, dad." Jonathon quietly offered as he sat down on the edge of a nearby chair. "You need anything else? Your phone? The paper?"

"I'm sure he has his phone on him," his mom quipped as she turned to walk back into the kitchen. Jonathon's empathy suddenly switched to his father. His dad was lying here in pain and his mother was acting like he deserved it.

Jonathon's dad felt around by his pants pocket to verify he had his phone. "You two go on. If I need anything, I can text you or your mother. Or…Lulu will be around. Don't mind me, I'm just going to lay here and let the heat and the Motrin kick in."

Just then Lulu piped in. "Jon-Jon made a machine he uses to help him relax and study. Maybe it could help you, Mr. Samuels." She gave a grin and a wink to Jonathon as his father lay with his eyes closed. The two of them then stared at each other, waiting for an answer.

"I don't know if I need that. You can tell me about your machine later, Jon. I think I just need to rest."

"Um…ya. I'll let you rest and maybe show you later if you want." He gave a thumbs-up to Lulu.

Jonathon then bolted upstairs. He needed to program his machine but hadn't really had time to conjure up what he wanted to input yet. Before he reached his room, he had a thought. He turned around and tip-toed down the stairs, watching to make sure his father still had his eyes closed. Then he slipped through the door off the entrance hall to enter his father's study. There was one entire wall of shelves filled with books. The ornate beauty of the wood along with a small hearth fireplace and easy chair gave the room an Old English warmth. When Jonathon was little, he often played on the carpeted floor by a crackling fire in the evenings while his father read, so he was very familiar with the room and went straight to a lower shelf to locate a particular photo album. He lowered himself to sit cross-legged on the floor in the corner and began thumbing through it for the first time in years.

Photos from when his parents dated filled the pages. One picture of his mom caught Jonathon's eye. She appeared to be trying on a wedding dress and was posing like a princess wearing her giant smile, something he hadn't seen for some time. He slipped the picture out of the sleeve and continued thumbing through. Many of the pictures had just his mother or his father. But he found one with both parents sitting on a blanket in a park somewhere. He thought it might be from their honeymoon. *They must have stopped someone passing by to take their picture together.* His mother sat gleaming at the camera and his father beaming at his mom. He pulled that photo out as well. Then he selected a few more before slipping the photo album back in its place. He stood up and carefully slid the photos into the back pocket of his jeans before sneaking out into the hallway. His father's snores could still be heard coming from the living room.

Once he got to his room, Jonathon took the photos out and slipped them into the scanner on the side of his machine. *What better way to remind them of the love that brought them together than seeing photos like these!* Jonathon thought. He opened his computer to research songs from his parents' school years and popular wedding songs from around the year they were married. Selecting a few that sounded familiar, he downloaded them into REMY.

He sat at his computer scratching his head, trying to think of what his parents used to enjoy doing together. He knew they used to love to go out with friends on weekends, remembering many nights he played Candyland or Chutes & Ladders with Lulu.

What else?

Jonathon heard a timid knock and his bedroom door slowly opened. Lulu poked her head around. "Sorry, Jon-Jon. Thought you'd want to know your mom just left."

"Thanks, Lulu. I'm almost ready." She started to close the door. "Hey, Lulu!" Jonathon muttered, just loud enough for her to hear. She poked her head back in. "What did my parents do when they went out…all those nights we used to play games and watch movies?"

Lulu took a step inside the door and gazed dreamily up at the ceiling as if there was a movie going on in her head. "Ah…I remember those days. They were so much fun! Little Jon-Jon and me always pretending we were camping or you helping me bake cookies in the kitchen…"

Jonathon waited a few seconds, feeling endeared she remembered those times so fondly. But he needed her to answer his question. "Lulu!"

She snapped out of her daydream and gave a giant smile to Jonathon. "Dancing. They loooooved dancing!" She started swaying as she said the words.

Jonathon sat back for a moment, remembering some of the high society functions he used to also attend. His parents ALWAYS found the dance floor before the end of the night. He then smiled and thanked Lulu before gently closing the door behind her.

About 20 minutes later, Jonathon was carefully navigating the stairs with his arms hugging the large machine. He was happy to find his father still sleeping soundly on the couch making small puffs with each breath. He quietly set his Machine on a couple of magazines lying on top of the coffee table. He then crawled around the side table and fumbled to find the outlet behind a curtain, so he could plug in REMY. Then ever so gently, he took the headphones from the holster and carefully slid them over his father's ears. His father stirred and then cleared his throat, never opening his eyes, and appeared to continue sleeping. Jonathon stood frozen for a moment before attaching the wires to the electrodes. He peeled off their adhesive backings and gently placed them on his dad's temples. His father was so out of it that Jonathon wondered if Motrin was all his mother had given him.

He turned on the Machine after making sure it was on mute. Then he gradually turned the volume up, just slightly so his dad wouldn't startle. When all was set up and running, Jonathon realized he was practically holding his breath. He inhaled deeply, quietly blowing out as he rose to slip out of the room. Lulu stood watching from the entrance, nibbling at her pinky nail intensely. She waved for Jonathon to follow her into the kitchen.

Once inside, they both tried to hush their uncontrollable laughter. "Man, I hope this works, Lulu!" he squeezed out between laughs. "I need to stay in here and keep watch through the door for when he wakes up."

"Okay…I will make a little snack for him before I start my pot roast. If he wakes up irritated, we can always distract him with food. I will make him some tea, too." Lulu scrunched up her shoulders and closed her eyes, sniffing the air as if the aroma of peppermint tea was already there. Then she turned to dutifully begin her meal prep.

Jonathon cracked the door open a few inches to make sure his dad was still sleeping and noticed him moving a little to adjust the heating pad. While subconsciously gritting his teeth, Jonathon watched his father scratch his nose, fold his hands over his stomach and grumble some undecipherable words, all while not fully waking.

When Jonathon felt his dad had settled, he pulled up a kitchen chair near the doorway where he could sit and watch. "So…are you getting anywhere with Mr. Mercado, Lulu?" He spoke just loud enough for her to hear, not taking his eyes from his father. She didn't respond immediately and Jonathon expected she wasn't going to give him much of an answer. He felt very surprised when Lulu began a detailed account of another encounter.

"Geez, Lulu. Are you stalking him? How much do you even know about him?"

"Well, I know he is YOUR teacher, Jon-Jon." At that Jonathon turned briefly to see her pointing her spatula at him.

He rolled his eyes and turned back around to keep watch. "Ya..." he whispered loudly. "...but what else? Is he married?"

"I don't think so. He doesn't wear no wedding ring." Jonathon thought for a moment and realized he had honestly never paid attention to that detail. "And he is always shopping by himself. And he shops for a dog." Jonathon snickered as he imagined her following the poor guy down the dog food aisle.

"Well...what else do you need to know then?" Jonathon tried to muffle a laugh. He then heard her muttering to herself, barely loud enough for Jonathon to hear. She was saying it was all Jon-Jon's fault.

After about 20 minutes, Jonathon felt his eyes getting heavy, struggling to keep them open. A moment before he was about to nod off, he observed his dad starting to squirm. Jonathon got up and walked into the living room, deliberately kicking the coffee table to make a noise. His father opened his eyes and started to sit up but retreated as he winced from his back pain. He immediately reached up to feel what was on his head, lifting the earphones from his head with a puzzled look on his face. Jonathon put out a hand to reach for them.

"How did those get on me?" his dad questioned. He seemed a little embarrassed that he didn't know.

"I thought you could use a little music to help you relax. How's your back?"

Jonathon leaned forward to peel off the electrodes as he studied his father's face. His dad sat still, eyeing Jonathon cautiously at first. Then, with obvious aggravation, he complained with another moan. "Where's the switch to this thing? It's too hot," he hollered, pulling the heating pad out from under his back and shoving it off the couch.

Jonathon flipped the switch on the chord to turn it off. "Did you like the music, dad?" he asked as he reached down to unplug his Machine.

"It might have helped me sleep," he grumbled. When Jonathon just stood there with an expressionless stare, his father sensed he should probably elaborate a little more. "It was nice…what kind of machine is that, son?"

"Ohhhh…just something I came up with. I use it when I need to really study and memorize things for a test or for a debate," Jonathon lied.

His dad nodded but Jonathon could tell from the grimaced look on his face that he was having a difficult time focusing on a conversation. Just then, Lulu came around the corner carrying a cup of tea. "Here, Mr. Samuels. Maybe this will help you relax even more. It's herbal."

Jonathon's dad tried to lean up enough to take a sip of the tea but handed it back to Lulu when it proved to be too difficult a task for him. He laid his head back down and closed his eyes. Jonathon knew he probably wouldn't get another opportunity to use REMY on his dad, so he picked up his Machine. "I'll just take this back up, so you can rest."

"Thanks, son. I appreciate your efforts." His dad was still a kind man, even in pain, and Jonathon hoped his intended intervention would somehow help his parents. He lugged the heavy Machine back up the stairs to its place and then collapsed on his bed. Though he knew he needed to work on homework, the heaviness of his eyelids began taking over. Homework would have to wait. Thoughts of Leana whirled around in his head and he wondered if she was spending time with Jasper again today. He thought of his mom out with her friends, seeming to have no interest in being at home to help her husband. Lastly, he thought of Lulu, and he chuckled out loud. Just before sleep consumed him, he thought of Kate and wondered what kind of dream she had that she couldn't even talk about.

Monday morning, Jonathon arrived at school wondering which direction his relationships might head this week with Jasper, Leana and Kate. He wasn't surprised to find Jasper missing from the vicinity of the lockers again. Waiting for a few minutes in case Jasper showed up, he saw Kendra Lake and Kate's best friend Mia walked past him in the hallway. They began whispering and giggling when they saw Jonathon. Feeling a little taken aback, he suspected Kate must have told THEM about her dream. He quickly turned to pretend he was looking for something in his locker.

When he got to class, Jasper was seated at a desk near the door, conveniently surrounded by occupied chairs. Jonathon rolled his eyes and scowled as he walked past. The two exchanged glances, Jasper giving a slight smile and "hey," but Jonathon barely acknowledging him. As soon as class was done, Jasper bolted out of the door and Jonathon decided he wouldn't bother trying to go after him this time. There wasn't much to say.

In the study hall, JR sat planted at his usual table with a group of male friends, including Jason Bon from the debate team. Even though the season was over, a wave of guilt washed over Jonathon when he saw Jason, realizing he hadn't been hanging out with his team lately. Being a co-team captain, he felt some responsibility in keeping the group cohesive during off season. As he passed their table, he avoided eye contact by scrolling to the calendar on his phone, taking a mental note of their next meeting. If JR hadn't been there, he would have joined Jason. Finding an empty table, he sat down, looking around. With no sign of Leana, he decided to take full advantage of the undistracted study time.

Later, when he arrived at his chemistry class, he was surprised to find Leana still absent, so he paired up with Reno Johnson who was also missing his project partner. When class was over, while walking out, he almost slammed into his old friend Sol and they both abruptly stopped, face to face in the crowd.

"Oh, hey, Sol. Sorry," Jonathon apologized.

"Jon! What's up?" Sol took a step back to ease the awkward closeness.

"Not much…so, how have you been?" The moment felt forced to Jonathon. The past several years they often passed each other by without any sign of recognition.

Sol let out a short guffaw. "I'm good, man. It's been a long time."

"Ya. I guess we just are both busy with…you know…stuff." Jonathon noticed Sol wearing his backpack with a skateboard poking out of the top. "I think I saw you in town on that thing," he said pointing to the board. "You're pretty good." Jonathon remembered when they first tried skateboarding in elementary school. "I never did catch on to it."

Sol whipped around and tilted his head to the side to keep his long hair out of his face. "It's my main mode of transportation," he laughed. "By the way, I remember your maid…what was her name…?"

"Lulu?" Jonathon asked, wondering why he brought her up.

"Ya. Lulu. She was really nice. Always making us cookies for our class, remember?" He pointed off in the distance as if that class was right down the hall. "So, I just saw her down by the art room with a plate of cookies. Just like old times!" With this he let out a chortle. "I was going to go up to her but thought…nah."

Jonathon's mouth fell open. Mr. Mercado's classroom was right next to the art lab. He recalled Lulu's brazen acts lately and again wondered what on Earth she must have dreamt to cause her persistent stalking of his teacher.

Raising his eyebrows, Jonathon shrugged, indicating he had no idea. "I don't think the cookies are for me," he chuckled. "Who knows who she's bribing." They both gave a little laugh and said goodbye. Jonathon felt good about chatting with Sol again, even briefly. He also felt a little melancholy that their lifestyles ultimately ended their friendship. As he dwelled a moment on a few memories, a sudden feeling of remorse hit him. *What if REMY destroys my relationship with Jasper?*

After school, Jonathon felt drained and was anxious to get home. Heading down the school steps, he tensed when Kate came jogging toward him with a huge smile on her face.

"Heyya," she gleamed.

"Hey, Kate, good day?" Jonathon returned the smile apprehensively.

"It was…okay." She gave a quirky face as they began walking together.

"You seem bubbly for it just being okay," Jonathon remarked to make conversation.

Her face then began to turn red. "I had another dream."

Jonathon stopped and turned toward her. "Are you NOT going to tell me this one either?"

Kate turned to continue walking, leading Jonathon to pick up his pace in order to keep up with her. "I didn't say it was about you. So…no." She cocked her head toward him in a flirty fashion.

"Fair enough," he said, somewhat relieved. They walked a few seconds in silence. Then he asked, "Why'd you even bother to tell me you had a dream, then?"

At first, she didn't answer. He felt she was trying to come up with an explanation. Then she was the one to stop. Jonathon halted and faced her. She looked up at him with a somewhat worried look on her face.

"I lied." She turned her eyes downward and began swaying nervously. "It WAS about you," she said, not looking up.

Jonathon bit his bottom lip while trying to think of what to say. He was enjoying her shy innocence. "Well…we're friends. Very good friends. You can tell me…if you want." She stopped swaying and looked up at him. Her eyes looked glassy as if she was about to cry.

Suddenly, Jonathon lost his amusement of the situation. "What's wrong, Kate? Did I die or something?"

Kate broke out laughing and crying at the same time. "No! It's nothing like that. It's just...I'm embarrassed to say...it was kind of..."

Just then, several kids passed by them on the sidewalk and Jonathon gently pulled her out of their path to keep their conversation private. "Let's keep walking." He put his hand on her back to direct her.

They walked a couple of minutes until they were almost at the corner where they normally went in separate directions. "It was..." She made a big sigh. "Romantic." She kept her head down and seemed to speed up her pace a little.

Jonathon smiled, feeling a genuine sense of endearment, but also nervous about her confession. She was clearly embarrassed, and he felt bad but the thought kind of intrigued him. He wished he could tell her why she was dreaming about him and about REMY but he needed to give that some serious consideration before admitting anything.

They came to a stop on the corner. "I think that's sweet, Katy Bear." He used the personal nickname he'd often called her and then reached out his arms to pull her in for a hug. "You don't need to be embarrassed. It was only a dream," he whispered above her head as he tried to put her at ease. They stood at the corner embraced as a crowd of students nudged around to use the crosswalk, ignoring them. Then, abruptly, Jonathon pushed back a little, so he could see her face. "Why don't I ever see you all day? I know we see each other in Spanish, but I haven't seen you at lunch in…forever." He was trying to break up the awkwardness with small talk.

Kate backed away and took a quick deep breath to compose herself before speaking. "I have Woodshop just before lunch and I usually stay and just eat a sandwich while I finish whatever I'm working on. And to clean up."

"Ohhhh ya. Woodshop. With your buddy JR." Jonathon's response sounded a little sarcastic and Kate gave him a frown.

"My buddy?" She balked.

Jonathon changed the subject again quickly, to get out of answering. "Did you find out when you are starting your new job?"

Kate paused as she eyed Jonathon curiously. She was wondering why he seemed irritated that she was friends with JR. "They want me to start training either tomorrow night or Wednesday night. I think I'll do it tomorrow. I'm hoping I can work Friday night instead of Saturday, so I can go to the dance." She searched his face for a moment to read his reaction.

"That'd be nice." Jonathon began to worry she might suggest they go to the dance together and quickly rushed his exit. "Well, I have a lot of homework. Didn't do as much as I'd hoped over the weekend. I'll catch ya later." He turned to leave.

Kate didn't move as he started walking away and she called out. "Are you going?"

Jonathon stopped and looked back at her. "Ya. Like I said, I have a lot of homework to do…"

"No. To the dance?" Kate rolled her eyes and tried to grin.

"Ohhhh. Yes, I think so. Hope you can go." Jonathon quickly turned back around and hurried to leave her and the conversation behind. The fact that Kate was dreaming about him was concerning but now he felt bad about being a little rude. He also realized his sarcasm about JR and knew she didn't deserve him taking out his frustrations on her. Resisting the urge to go back to apologize, he instead tried to redirect his thoughts back toward Leana and how he was going to get her to come back to his house.

The next day in chemistry, Jonathon was pleased to see Leana back in class and was excited to talk to her. After a 20-minute lecture from Mr. Bell, the students broke up into their lab groups. Leana seemed thoughtful as she approached Jonathon.

"Hi." She grinned and set her notebook down on the lab table. "Thanks again for the notes. You're very thorough."

Jonathon took it as a compliment but still apologized with a chuckle. "Sorry, I can be a little detail-oriented. But I hope they'll help."

"Oh…I'm glad you are! I'll probably do better on this next exam than any others this year."

"Good. I hope so." Jonathon began pulling out instruments and the Bunsen burner to set up. Then he noticed Jason Bon's lab partner was still absent and felt obligated to invite him to work with them. He really wanted to be alone with Leana but felt he had no choice. As it turned out, Jason added a pleasant vibe with his humorous banter. The three of them laughed a lot and worked together happily, giving Jonathon relief from coming up with conversation.

When they were cleaning up and packing their backpacks, Leana leaned closer to Jonathon when Jason had left the table. "So… that Machine of yours?" Jonathon tensed with a worried anticipation. "Jasper told me to stay away from it."

Jonathon felt his blood beginning to boil. *What a dog!* he thought, now angrier than ever at Jasper. "Why would he say that?" he shot back at Leana, his thoughts scurrying for an additional rebuttal.

"I don't know," Leana took a step back. "He just said I should stay away and wouldn't tell me why." Leana made direct eye contact with her next question. "So…you tell me Jon. Why WOULD he say that?"

Now he felt cornered. He picked up his backpack and said with a huff, "Maybe he's just jealous that he doesn't have a Machine like it!" Then he turned and left the room. He couldn't wait to see Jasper to give him a piece of his mind.

Unfortunately for Jonathon, Jasper continued to avoid him, and he didn't see him the rest of the day. He knew Jasper must have known Leana would say something to him.

In the afternoon when Jonathon got home, Lulu seemed excited to greet him as he came into the kitchen.

"Hello, Jon-Jon!" I didn't see you yesterday after school and I was busy last night. How are things?" She gave a nod of her head to a bouquet of flowers sitting on the middle of the table.

Jonathon was about to answer her question when he saw the flowers. He walked over and reached for the already opened notecard stuck in the middle of them. He read the card out loud.

I HOPE YOU HAVE A NICE DAY. YOUR JON

Jonathon looked up at Lulu in disbelief. "These are for my mom? From dad?!"

Lulu gave a slow mischievous nod with a sly grin. "And…he even gave her a little peck goodbye this morning!" she added.

"Oh…my…God!" Jonathon emphasized each word with a pause between. The two of them then started dancing around the kitchen giving high fives and laughing. When they heard footsteps coming down the stairs, they both sobered their demeanor and Jonathon sat down for breakfast as Lulu turned toward the stove.

Mrs. Samuels came in the kitchen door looking quite happy. "Good morning, Jonathon! Did you see my lovely flowers?" She was beaming.

Jonathon gave a quick glance at Lulu who still had her back to them before he answered. "Yes. As a matter of fact, I couldn't miss them. How nice, mom! It's not your anniversary or anything, is it?" He knew it wasn't.

"No. No. That's the nice thing. It's just a sweet gesture." She stood deep in thought, smiling at the flowers for a few seconds.

Jonathon thought he heard Lulu murmur just loud enough for him to hear. "It's about time."

As they ate their breakfast, Jonathon was dying to ask Lulu about her cookie delivery she'd made to the school the day before. But, not wanting to embarrass her, he decided to leave it alone for the time being.

Jonathon decided to take a little different route to school in hopes of crossing paths with Jasper. There wasn't a cloud in the sky and a cool, light breeze felt good against his face. He was in a good frame of mind until he rounded the corner near the school and spotted Jasper standing with a small group of students. Jonathon hadn't really rehearsed what he wanted to say to him but he knew he had to address Jasper's betrayal.

He came up behind Jasper and surprised him when he belted out, "We need to talk." Jasper whipped around looking frightened.

"Hey, Jon," he replied nervously. The two walked away from the other students who simply continued talking amongst themselves, paying no attention to Jasper's exit.

When they got over to a grassy area away from others, Jonathon turned to Jasper and let his backpack drop from his hand onto the ground. He leaned in with both of his arms stiffened at his sides. "You are some friend!" he scowled. "I thought you were my best friend! I get it that my Machine caused you to dream about Leana…and I was actually feeling this whole situation was my fault, but then you went and told her about my Machine!"

"Hey…wait a minute! I did NOT tell her about your machine! I mean…" He put up two fingers with each hand signaling quotation marks. "REMY." He tried to chuckle but quickly dropped his hands when he saw the scornful look on Jonathon's face. "YOU had her over to your house and YOU showed her the machine." He then slowly pronounced each syllable. "Re-mem-ber?!"

Jonathon was seething. "But YOU told her to stay away from my Machine!"

"Well, SHE asked ME if I knew about it! What was I supposed to say? I just told her to stay away from it. I didn't tell her what you planned to do with it!" Jasper was now the one feeling hot under the collar.

"I'm sorry I ever confided in you at all!" Jonathon screamed. "I thought I could trust you!" The two stood there not really looking at each other as a few students were now noticing the commotion. Jonathon began pacing over a small patch of grass to calm down.

Jasper was still looking down and had his hands in his pockets. Then he spoke with an unapologetic tone. "I'm not sorry. I really, really like her, Jon." Jonathon felt a cloud of panic roll through him, realizing Jasper was now as mesmerized with Leana as he was.

Jonathon picked up his backpack and threw it over his shoulder. "I don't even know what to say." With that, he stormed off leaving Jasper looking disheartened.

The rest of the day Jonathon felt he was in a daze. A quiz in chemistry class took most of the period and he barely said hello to Leana, or anyone else for that matter. He finished the test well ahead of most of the students and was allowed to leave. He tried making eye contact with Leana as he quietly left the classroom, but she never looked up.

He went back to his locker and considered leaving a note for Jasper but really didn't have anything to say. Instead, he hurried outside to beat the rush of students that would stampede the grounds once the bell rang. He secured a shady spot under a large sycamore tree and plopped down to sit with his back against the tree trunk, pulling out a sandwich Lulu had made for him. Happy to be alone with his thoughts, he juggled in his head what he should do about the calamity he had created. When the bell rang, a flood of kids came streaming out the doors scattering in various directions. He decided to push his thoughts away and pulled out his English workbook to finish up some homework. He found himself momentarily nodding off a few times but the heaviness of his head jerking quickly awakened him.

Just before the bell signaling the end of lunch rang, he glanced up to see Kate jogging toward him. As she approached, she was slightly out of breath and had tiny sweat beads dotting her forehead. She came to a stop and threw her backpack on the ground.

"Phew. It's actually hot out here. I thought I'd come find you since you said you never see me during the day. I finished Woodshop a little early so I could."

Jonathon shielded the sun from his eyes as he looked up at her and then stood to brush some grass from his pant legs. "That's nice of you." He wondered if she had news of another dream but he didn't dare ask. "You want me to walk you to class…you have English now, right?"

"If you have time." She turned to begin walking and Jonathon noticed how cute she looked in her one-piece jumpsuit. "I started my job last night!" she proclaimed giddily.

"Oh, that's right! How'd it go?"

"JR's aunt is super nice. Betty. She taught me how the books are categorized and showed me how to log in shipments. Stuff like that. Oh, and she showed me how to use the register but I haven't used it yet. Anyway, it was super fun. Jasper came in."

Jonathon sneered at the sound of his name but Kate didn't notice since he continued to walk behind her. "Oh, did he? And what was he looking for?" He fought the urge to ask if Jasper was looking for a book on friendship. Kate wouldn't have understood his sarcasm anyway, and it would have led to her asking questions that he didn't want to answer.

"I don't know. He just came in…and said hi. He was looking around."

"By himself?" Jonathon couldn't resist the chance to satisfy his curiosity since the opportunity arose.

Kate tilted her head and looked up slightly, thinking out loud. "Let me see…I… I think so. He might have been talking to someone else before he left. I was busy, absorbing everything Betty was telling me, so I wasn't really paying too much attention."

They slowed down as they approached the door to her English class. Kate hesitated before going in and turned to look up at Jonathon. "JR says he wants to go to the dance, and he asked if I was going." She raised her eyebrows and Jonathon wondered why she was telling him this. He again felt agitated, suppressing a snide remark.

"Are you glad…that he is going? Or that he asked you if you were?"

Kate stood looking up into Jonathon's eyes. She didn't say anything at first, making him feel uneasy with her prolonged eye contact. Without saying a word, she seemed to be asking him for more of a response than he had just given. Finally, not batting an eye she replied, "I guess I should be." She scrunched her mouth up and looked to be biting the inside of her lip. Then she turned to walk inside.

Jonathon leaned over her to hold the door open as she slid under his arm to enter. "OK. Well, I'll maybe see you on the walk home." He wasn't sure that was what she wanted to hear.

She turned around wearing a disappointed look on her face and gave a quick wave as she continued toward a desk. "Sure." Then the door clicked shut in front of him.

In American Government, Jonathon had little time to worry about Kate's odd vibe during the earlier lunch break. A discussion on the death penalty led by Mr. Kip took an odd turn toward the subject of human cloning. With most of his debate team being in class, the ideas and exchanges between the students made the time go by fast. Then, in Spanish class, there was a substitute teacher, so the students broke up into small groups to practice their conversational skills. Jonathon laughed to himself as he pictured Mr. Mercado tied up to a chair by Lulu somewhere. Then looking around the room it dawned on him Kate hadn't shown up for class.

On the walk home, there was still no sign of Kate. Jonathon stopped to hang out at "their corner" for a few minutes, hoping he might run into her. He had a weird feeling about how she had left him after lunch. Waiting for about 5 minutes, he gave up and continued in the direction of his house, glancing back a time or two to see if he could spot her. He never did.

When Jonathon was almost home, he remembered his plans to join a gym. He knew of one about 10 blocks away and decided today was as good as any day. It was a small, privately owned, non-franchised gym called Jim's Gym. When he arrived, no one was at the front desk. He leaned on the counter as he waited. The walk in the warm afternoon sun had left his back sweaty, so the air-conditioned room felt good.

It didn't take long before a very muscular, middle-aged man came through a door located behind the desk. Beyond the opened door, Jonathon could see a few people working out on various machines in a large room behind him.

"Can I help you? I'm Jim."

Jonathon reached out to shake his hand and as Jim grabbed it, Jonathon was caught off guard by his strong grip and quickly tried to adjust his own to match his. "I'm Jon. Um, I'm interested in joining a gym and thought I'd check out your place."

"Welcome! You live locally?"

"Yes." Jonathon pointed in the direction he'd just walked. "Not far. I walked here actually."

"Great. Well, come on back. I'll show you around, buddy."

Jonathon followed his motion to come around the desk and they entered the large workout area. There were several rows of machines and one half of the room had mats with medicine balls and free weights on shelves lining the wall. Only three people were using the equipment, no one Jonathon recognized. He liked this atmosphere better than the ones he had seen advertised, with massive workout classes and garden cafés for socializing. All he wanted was to build a little muscle without all the fanfare.

After a short tour of the locker room, showers and a sauna area, Jim asked Jonathon if he had any questions. Jonathon felt a little embarrassed but asked if someone could show him how each machine worked. He felt relieved to hear a trainer would give him more details and could set him up with a program on his first visit if he joined. The vibe felt comfortable to Jonathon, and he liked Jim. Without a further thought or hesitation, he signed a few waivers and received a contract for his parents to sign, then scheduled his first training session for the upcoming Saturday morning at 11:00 a.m.

Walking back home, Jonathon had a little pep in his step as he imagined himself with a more muscular build. He walked with a smile on his face, picturing Leana reaching and squeezing his forearm while commenting, with a gleam in her eye, on how strong he is. *Maybe this will be my next dream*, he thought. He then chuckled a bit, imagining Kate discovering he was now working out. She would be amused.

Jonathon walked into his house and spotted Lulu on a step stool putting a picnic basket away in the hall closet. She was wearing light pink lipstick and a floral sundress with flip flops. She turned to look over her shoulder at Jonathon who was approaching her.

"Need some help, Lulu?" Jonathon eyed the picnic basket suspiciously.

"No. I got it," she whimpered as she strained to shove the basket onto a shelf barely within her reach while on her tiptoes.

"You should be careful in those flip flops on that stool!" Jonathon gently laid his hand against her back as she stepped off. "An afternoon outing?"

She gave him a side-eyed glance with a mischievous grin and then reached down to pick up the stool. "If you're being Mr. Nosybody, I will tell you." She stood up and before doing an about face to enter the kitchen with the stool in hand she confidently stated, "I had a date."

Jonathon reacted with a half-surprised look on his face. "Wow!" Then the realization hit him and he followed her into the kitchen. "So…is that why Mr. Mercado had a substitute?" He threw his backpack onto the kitchen counter and put both hands on his hips as he started to laugh. "You two were playing hooky!"

Lulu swung around and put her finger up to her lips hoping to hush him. "Our secret, Jon-Jon." You keep my secret and I'll keep yours," she said playfully.

Just then they heard the door from the garage open and a few seconds later Jonathon's mom came strolling in with a few shopping bags. "Good afternoon, you two!" She was setting her bags down when she noticed they were recovering from a laugh together. "Hope I'm not interrupting anything." She reached inside one of the shopping bags and didn't appear to really want an answer. Then she pulled out a bottle of FEVER cologne. "I got this for you, Jon. Your father said you borrowed some of his cologne and I thought this one was nice…" She opened the cap and gave it a little squirt into the air before leaning forward to sniff the falling spray. "The lady in the department store said a lot of the young men like it." She thrust the bottle under Jonathon's nose. "What do you think? Mmm." She closed her eyes as she inhaled again. "I really like it a lot. I was tempted to get your father some."

Jonathon felt the blood draining from his face. He tried to hide his humiliation, knowing his father was aware he'd snagged some of his cologne. "Thanks, mom." He gave her a big hug and after taking in the scent, he told her he liked it.

"Oh, Lulu! Before I forget, Mr. Samuels and I won't be home for dinner tomorrow. So don't plan on us." His mother seemed to be on Cloud Nine.

Lulu turned around and looked at Jonathon with a wink and a subtle thumbs-up, which she hid from his mother.

"That's great, mom." Jonathon said warmly. "You and dad going out?"

"Yes! And he even cancelled his plans with the guys to spend time with me…" She turned on her heels as she grabbed the shopping bags. "…for no good reason." She sauntered out the kitchen door and headed for the stairs. Jonathon and Lulu stood looking at each other in amazement.

Lulu put her hand on her hip in her usual Lulu style and remarked, "That's one heck of a machine you built there, Jon-Jon!"

On Friday, the student body chatter was all about the upcoming dance. A committee planned deliveries of potted plants and small trees to the gymnasium from the locally owned Plant Palace. Jonathon spotted Kate's friend Mia, Kendra Lake and a few other girls standing at the entrance to the gym with clipboards. Mia appeared to be in charge, organizing the crew and directing a couple of guys carrying boxes labeled ***Italian String Lights*** to a far corner. Other student volunteers were rhythmically passing by carrying individual pots of flowers from a truck backed up to the side entrance. Jonathon walked over by the gym doors to peek inside. Since he had never been to a dance, he found it intriguing to watch the work put forth for the event.

A rush of nerves churned in his stomach at the thought of actually being at the dance the next night. *What if Leana doesn't even show up? Or worse yet, what if she shows up with Jasper!* Jonathon's thoughts caused him to shudder as he felt resentment building toward his best friend. Jasper had gone to a few of dances in the past, so Jonathon felt it likely he'd at least show up now that he liked Leana. *I need to keep Jasper from going tomorrow night.*

A moment later, Kate walked up next to Jonathon, brushing Jonathon's arm with her sweater, breaking his dazed fixation. "It's amazing what they do for these dances." She smiled sweetly, not looking directly at Jonathon but staring out at the pod of plants still clustered in the middle of the gym.

"I was just thinking the same thing." He surveyed Kate while contemplating what might be going on in her head.

Still not looking up at her friend, Kate muttered "I can't say I never see you at school now." She then turned toward the group from the dance committee. "Hey, Mia."

With that, she took a few steps in their direction, no longer acknowledging Jonathon.

He stood a moment, stunned by her flippant remark. Then figuring Kate to be in one of those "moods" girls seemed to get into from time to time, he turned to leave for class. Rounding a corner, Jasper passed by him in the hall, huddled in a whispered conversation with Kendra Lake. If he noticed Jonathon, he did a good job hiding it. "Great!" Jonathon said out loud as he continued toward his locker. "Now he's getting chummy with Leana's friends."

When last period Spanish class rolled around, Jonathon felt eager to have the school week come to an end. While taking notes, he watched Mr. Mercado closely. His teacher always gave personal attention to each student and displayed a magnetic personality around campus. So, Jonathon could see why Lulu liked him, but he found it outright flabbergasting Lulu was able to charm his teacher in just over one week, enough to convince him to ditch a class for her.

Mr. Mercado came up to Jonathon as the bell rang. "Jon." He looked up and saw his teacher standing and wringing his hands looking nervous. "I guess you know that I met your housekeeper, Lulu?"

Jonathon slipped out of his desk and stood, so he could have a conversation more comfortably. "Um, yes. She mentioned she met you…a couple of times." He held back details, not wanting to embarrass his teacher by revealing everything he knew.

"Well, I've asked her to come chaperone the dance with me tomorrow night. She filled out a waiver and got fingerprinted at the office, so I think she'll be there. She told me you were going, so I wanted you to know…." His voice trailed off.

"Oh." Jonathon was at a loss for words. "Okay…ya. That's great, I guess."

"Unless it makes you uncomfortable…" Mr. Mercado sensed Jonathon's reluctance and stood with his hands folded together as if he was praying.

Jonathon fought off a laugh, thinking he resembled a little kid asking permission. "No. No. That's fine. I…" he raised his eyebrows. "....whatever you want to do. It doesn't bother me."

"You know…she's been a breath of fresh air. I haven't gotten out much the last year and a half since my wife passed and…" he began to get choked up and pulled a tissue from his pocket to wipe his eyes. Then he gave a nervous laugh. "Sorry. It's still hard to talk about."

"Gosh, Mr. Mercado. I had no idea. I'm sorry." Jonathon suddenly felt a deep gratitude for having Lulu fall victim to REMY's magic.

"Thanks, bud." Mr. Mercado patted Jonathon's shoulder and turned to go back to his desk.

The classroom was empty except for the two of them as Jonathon was leaving. He stopped at the doorway on the way out. "You know, Mr. Mercado…I think the world of Lulu. She's really a great lady. I'm glad you're getting to know her."

"Thanks, Jon." He nodded appreciatively. "See you at the dance."

Secretly, Jonathon wasn't exactly thrilled to have Lulu watching his every move at his first dance. He knew she would be feeling excited, getting to watch her Jon-Jon stumble over his feet and possibly make a fool of himself while trying to impress a girl. If he was lucky, she'd be gushing over Mr. Mercado instead of watching him.

While at his locker, Jonathon began to come up with a plan. He could crush up a couple of allergy pills containing an antihistamine and put them in a smoothie for Jasper. If he timed it right, Jasper would become so sleepy he'd take a long nap and oversleep, missing the dance. Jonathon left school still considering that possibility, but realizing how unsafe it could be, and probably illegal, he nixed the idea. Then walking home, he came up with another. He could tell Jasper's parents some kind of lie, causing Jasper to get grounded. Quickly, he dismissed that option. It wasn't in his nature to be that deceitful. Besides, he respected Jasper's parents too much to involve them. *There has to be something else I can do,* he thought.

Still walking toward home, Jonathon was in his own little dream world and didn't realize, until he was right on the heels of a small group of girls ahead, that Kate was one of them.

"Kate!" Jonathon hollered, not meaning to get the whole group's attention, but he did, and they all turned around. Kate wove between two of the girls to come back to walk with Jonathon.

"I wanted to talk to you. Are you okay?" he cautiously asked. "I'm sensing you're kinda mad at me." One of the girls up ahead overheard and turned her head slightly to listen in, so Jonathon and Kate both slowed to let the group keep some distance.

Once they dropped back a few more feet, Kate shook her head as she spoke. "Nope, Jon. I am not mad." She took a deep breath. "I'm sorry if I am acting weird. It's hard to explain."

Jonathon wasn't sure he wanted to push any further to discover her meaning. When they reached the corner, he held his arms out to give her a big hug. "I don't want you to ever be mad at me."

Kate rocked quietly in his arms but didn't lift her own. She was holding onto her backpack straps, afraid to show any emotion. When Jonathon released his embrace, he gently gripped both of her small shoulders and looked down at her, perplexed.

"Whatcha got going on tonight, Kate Bear?" he asked, trying to lighten up the unusual awkwardness between them.

She turned her head, not looking at Jonathon. Instead, she gazed down the road back toward the school, appearing to be lost in thought. When her non-committed gaze turned to one of recognition, Jonathon turned to see what she was looking at. He spotted JR about 20 yards away, leaning against a tree texting on his phone.

Kate looked at Jonathon to finally answer his question. "Um... nothing fun. Just working," she quickly replied taking a step away, causing Jonathon to drop his arms from her. "Sorry. I need to catch JR," she said, shuffling off.

Jonathon, feeling irked by the situation, quickly headed home. *This guy is really getting to feel like a thorn in my side,* he thought.

* * * *

The house was quiet when Jonathon walked in. A note with dinner instructions for heating up a small pot pie was posted on the refrigerator door by a golf-bag magnet. Not yet hungry enough for dinner, Jonathon eyed the counter for a snack and found a plate of brownies wrapped in foil. He grabbed two with a napkin and trudged upstairs. Tomorrow was the dance, so this evening he would program a great dream of the two of them intended for her. And though he had yet to come up with an exact plan for how, he'd somehow pull her away from the dance to come to his house. He sat down at his desk and went to work.

It was almost 7:00 p.m. when he woke up with his head slouched on his arm atop his desk. He had spent about an hour creating a dream for Leana and then studied Spanish before mental fatigue got the best of him. He sat up, stretching his arms overhead. As he slowly twisted his neck to each side, trying to sluff off his grogginess, he began to recall a dream he just had while napping. He was in his chemistry class and instead of Leana, Kate was seated at a table next to him. She was working on a project with JR, and Jonathon was trying to ask her a question, only Kate couldn't hear him. He was trying to get out of his chair to approach her, but his legs were heavy and wouldn't move. His frustration was mounting when JR turned toward him but it suddenly wasn't JR's face, it was Jasper's.

Jonathon stood up to shake the strange dream from his head before jogging down the stairs to go heat up his dinner.

It felt odd to not have anyone in the house. Lulu was almost always home but Jonathon now speculated she had some mischievous plans, again with Mr. Mercado. Just a few short weeks ago, she was happy to spend her evenings watching game shows or a movie.

After eating, Jonathon changed into a pair of gray jeans and a long-sleeved, light blue pullover before brushing his teeth. He went back downstairs, plopping onto the living room couch. He turned on the television and scrolled through the guide. Nothing looked interesting enough to distract his preoccupied mind and he turned the TV off. Feeling a little fresh air would do him good, he decided to take a walk into town.

As dusk morphed into darkness, the temperature outside began to drop, and the night sky was beginning to glitter with stars. Their illumination was more brilliant as he took a shortcut to town through an alley void of streetlights. He was humming a tune and walking with his hands in his pockets to keep warm. Emerging onto the main street, Jonathon rounded the corner to head toward the most vibrant area of town. He was immediately met by a group of four guys who seemed to just be hanging out. Three of the four had a cigarette hanging from their lips. The fourth was holding an e-pen. They all turned to face Jonathon as he slowed his gait and tried to figure out the best way to get around them.

"Hey, dude. What's going on?" One of the taller guys gave a sly smirk and took a step toward Jonathon. "You're looking like you have somewhere important to be." The guy then turned back around to the other three. "Doesn't he look mighty fine?" They all snickered and nodded in agreement.

Jonathon, feeling tense, took his hands out of his pockets and tried standing a little straighter. "Just headed to town, guys." He held his position, looking straight into the eyes of his inquisitor, trying not to look fearful. He contemplated whether he could outrun the group but figured running should be his last resort.

"I bet you have a little dough on you…that you can loan us. You know, a little something to help us have some fun tonight?" With that question, Jonathon realized he might be in serious trouble. He didn't want to give these dudes his money, but he also didn't want to end up somewhere in a ditch or in the bushes.

Jonathon felt panicked to be so outnumbered but before he had time to cower and turn over his money, he noticed a few guys across the street on the opposite corner. One was Sol. He normally would have avoided him and his group, but Jonathon wanted nothing more than to rid himself of the threatening gang and hollered out as loud as he could. "Hey, Sol!"

Sol turned and saw Jonathon jetting across the street toward him. "Heyyy!" Sol greeted him with a low five and a smack on the back as he glanced past Jonathon at the corner from where he had just escaped. "Those dudes giving you trouble?" he joked.

"Haaa. No. They just wanted my money, that's all." He wiped his forehead with his sleeve as he tried to laugh it off.

Sol turned to yell back to the gang. "Hey!" All four guys looked up to see Sol wrapping an arm around Jonathon's neck and patting his chest with his other hand. "This is my long-lost friend. Back off!" He pointed at the group and gave them a thumbs-up. The group across the street waved Sol and Jonathon off as if shooing them away before they turned their backs again snickering. Only their leader stared them down for a moment before taking a drag of his cigarette and blowing a circle into the night air just to show he didn't really care whether Jonathon was Sol's friend or not.

Jonathon turned to Sol. "Hey…thank you," he paused, "…for being a friend." He reached out and shook Sol's hand. "I hope I can repay the favor someday."

"Well, you know where you can find me if you ever want to just hang out," Sol quipped. The encounter with Sol was brief but it made Jonathon feel good. He sensed Sol felt as happy for their friendship as Jonathon did at that moment.

Making his way into the town center, Jonathon spotted a lone guitarist who was sitting on a bench next to the bus stop, playing covers of popular artists. Not having any agenda, Jonathon slowed to a stop and listened until the musician finished playing a song. Then he pulled out his wallet and found a dollar bill to toss into the open guitar case. Before tossing it in, he considered how lucky he was to still have his wallet. So, he dug further to find a five-dollar bill and tossed it in instead. The artist had begun playing again and gave a nod of thanks.

Jonathon continued walking. As he was crossing the street approaching The Coffee Couch, he spotted JR in the distance coming out of the bookstore. Jonathon stopped. He was planning to go in for a coffee drink but decided to eavesdrop on JR and his group of friends who were standing around the popular hangout area. Jonathon paced back and forth near the corner, pretending he was waiting for someone. He listened intently, hoping to hear if JR mentioned Kate or Leana, but was unable to make out anything over the chatter and laughter coming from other students in the area.

After a few frustrating minutes, he was just about to lose interest when JR let out a bellowing laugh and turned his head to look down the street. Jonathon looked toward the group and drew in a deep breath when he noticed JR's jacket collar flipped downward, revealing a giant hickey on the side of JR's neck. Hickeys weren't that unusual, especially on Monday mornings following weekend dates, but wondering if the hickey may have come from Kate turned Jonathon's stomach. He no longer felt like hanging around and took off toward the bookstore to see if Kate was working, feeling agitated.

A set of bells attached to the door handle jangled as Jonathon turned the knob to walk in. Several kids from Cascadia High and a few younger middle-schoolers were browsing books, sipping drinks purchased from next door. A few girls stood huddled in the aisle, chatting in hushed tones. Jonathon walked past them toward the back where the register was located. He didn't see Kate at first and wondered if she truly was working there. He stood next to the counter eyeing the trinkets displayed in a case. For some reason, a miniature of Harry Potter and Hermione riding on a broomstick caught his eye and his thoughts turned to Jasper and Leana. He wondered if they were together tonight …or if Leana still liked JR. Another thought came to him. *JR's hickey may have come from Leana…or someone else, not Kate.* His mind was stirring, and he pondered whether he should warn Kate…*in case she IS interested in JR*. Unsure what to do, he suddenly felt uncomfortable about confronting her. He decided it best if he just went home but as he turned to leave, she was blocking his way, looking mighty with one hand on her hip and wearing a dark green apron that read *JUNIPER BOOKS*. Her name tag had small Juniper berries in the corner next to her name written out in calligraphy.

Kate tried to act professional in a teasing way. "Can I help you, sir?" she giggled.

"Hey, Katie Bear." He cleared his throat to change his demeanor. "I mean, why yes, ma'am. I am looking for someone… not a book." He gave her a grin.

"And…would that someone be me?" she winked in fun.

"I think that's a possibility." Jonathon kept up with her playfulness, all while continuing to contemplate whether he should bring up JR and his hickey. "Actually, I was just roaming the streets, bored. I remembered you were working."

"Oh, ya. I came in to cover the last half of the shift for JR. He's been helping out his aunt. And tomorrow I'm..." Just then a customer came walking up and interrupted them, asking Kate for help. Kate turned to Jonathon and whispered, "Sorry...catcha later," making a half-grin, appearing disappointed. Her eyes looked deep aqua tonight, reflecting the color of her apron, and momentarily captured Jonathon's attention. She quickly turned away and headed down the aisle as he watched her from a distance, maturely selecting books for the inquiring patron. Feeling proud of her and simultaneously sad he couldn't spend a little more time visiting, he left the store and stood outside in the cool evening air watching her through the window for a moment. *Why do I feel so nervous asking her about JR*? he questioned himself, chalking it up to his dislike for the guy and the fact they ran out of time to chat.

Once Kate was off helping others and no longer in his view, Jonathon headed to The Coffee Couch next door for the drink he meant to get earlier. There was no sign of Jasper or Leana. Even JR and his buddies had departed. Slipping inside, the room buzzed with chatter and whispers from every corner and the subdued lighting gave off a warm and comfortable vibe. The only faces he recognized were a few kids from his debate team. Reno, Sarah Jonday, Susan Shooflee and two others were seated at a table against the back wall. There was one open chair that could be his. Initially, he wanted to attempt a covert escape. After all, he had the challenging task of developing a plan for the dance tomorrow night and could use a little extra sleep. But a few of the group spotted him and waved him to come over. He figured he could sleep in and plan things in the morning instead.

After ordering an iced mocha, he wove through the groups seated on sofas and ottomans to reach the back table. When he slid into the empty seat next to the familiar group, they seemed enthused to have him join them. Even the unfriendly Susan Shooflee.

****

The following morning, Jonathon was slowly waking up as he heard the reverberating churn of a distant lawnmower. He was coming out of a dream. Leana was running on the school track, her long, wavy hair flowing behind her. He was running behind her trying to catch up and calling her name, but she never turned around. Then he looked up into the stands and saw Kate reading a book and wondered why she'd even be there if she wasn't watching the track and field event. As Jonathon slipped out of the dream, a wave of excitement hit him, remembering the dance. He stretched his arms and rolled over, coming in direct view of REMY. Suddenly, he realized the dream he'd programmed the night before hadn't come out quite like he programmed and he sat up in bed, irritated.

Planting his feet on the ground, he leaned over and stared at the floor thinking of how he was going to keep Jasper away from the dance. He was tired of his friend throwing wrenches into his months-long pursuit of Leana. Throwing his head back on his pillow, he closed his eyes. Suddenly, he remembered an idea that came to him while hanging out with his debate team the night before. Sarah

Jonday had told a story about her grandparents' plum farm and how they dried them to make prunes. When she was younger and stayed at their house one summer, she ventured into their small warehouse on the property and helped herself to the delicious, dried fruit, so much so that she spent much of the remainder of the day in the bathroom, not realizing prunes are a natural laxative. The group found her story quite funny and all of them had a good laugh. Only now that he was fully awake did he remember that while they were laughing, and sharing childhood memories, he sat quietly conjuring up a mischievous plan.

He bolted upright again and grabbed his phone from his desk to text Leana.

Hey Leana. I hope my notes were helpful this week.

He had decided it best to stay friendly with her. This might be the only way he could possibly get her over to his house again to finally use his Machine.

Then he texted Jasper.

I hate us fighting. Can I come by this afternoon?

Jonathon jumped in the shower while waiting for a response from either or both of them. When he got out, he checked his phone. He'd only heard back from Jasper.

Sure. I want to talk to you anyway.

"Great," Jonathon spewed out loud. He didn't really want to hear more about Jasper's feelings for Leana. He just needed to see him to carry out his plan. He quickly replied that he'd come by around five o'clock, then threw his phone onto his bed and strolled downstairs.

Lulu was in the living room vacuuming when Jonathon reached the lower level. She turned off the vacuum when she saw him heading into the kitchen and yelled out, "I just cleaned up. There's a muffin in the warming drawer and a bowl of fruit in the refrigerator if you want."

Jonathon leaned back outside the kitchen door. "Where's mom and dad? What time *IS* it?" He hadn't noticed the time on his phone while texting.

Lulu was moving the coffee table over and grunted. "I don't know. Somewhere between breakfast and lunch!" She turned the vacuum back on, ending their conversation.

Jonathon walked into the kitchen, grabbed the muffin and then took several minutes making a cappuccino with the complicated machine his father received on his last birthday. While he was waiting for his drink to finish brewing, he took a bite, closing his eyes and savoring the taste of the warm, homemade blueberry muffin on his tongue. He slouched into the dinette chair as he viewed the wall clock directly in front of him. It was almost 10:00 a.m. and Jonathon let out a gasp when he realized how late he'd slept, sending him into a coughing fit as he inhaled a small piece of blueberry. Taking a napkin, he wiped off his mouth and grabbed the muffin and coffee before quickly running upstairs to his room. An alarm was sounding on his phone, the one he had set to remind himself of his upcoming gym appointment. As he turned it off, he checked his messages, disappointed Leana had not responded yet.

Digging through his dresser drawers for something to wear, he began taking his frustration out on the perfectly folded clothes by throwing them into a disheveled pile on the floor. He finally chose some tennis shorts and an old tee shirt and quickly changed. Not owning a gym bag, Jonathon decided to empty the books and papers from his backpack onto his bed but then stood wondering what he was supposed to put in it. He rushed down to the kitchen to fill a water bottle and placed the one item in the backpack. Hoping he wasn't forgetting to take something vital, he suddenly remembered the waiver he left out for his mom to sign. He breathed a sigh of relief when he glanced over at the kitchen nook where he left it. She had signed it and left a note attached with a paperclip asking him to tell her about the gym later. He shoved the waiver in his pocket, grabbed his backpack and shouted a hurried goodbye to Lulu before setting out in a half-jog toward his destination.

Jonathon slowed down to cool off once he was a block away and realized he still had a few minutes until his appointment. The jog was more of a workout than he usually got on an average day. He began to feel a little nervous, anticipating what Jim had in store for his first session. He took off his eyeglasses and pulled his phone out of his pocket, placing them in a side pocket of his backpack. *Now I get why I need a gym bag.*

When he finally cooled off, he opened the door to walk inside, trying to act like he knew what he was doing. A tall girl now occupied the previously empty reception area. She had her back to Jonathon and was writing in a notebook. As the door clicked shut behind him, the girl turned around.

"Oh! Hi, Jon." She noticed a stunned look on Jonathon's face and felt the need to reintroduce herself. "Kendra." She gave him a grin, standing behind a desktop computer, typing as she talked. "Remember? We met last week briefly."

Jonathon knew exactly who she was and remained dazed with a million things running through his head. He hadn't planned on seeing anyone he knew, especially not a friend of Leana's. She quickly continued, to clarify her recognition. "I saw your name on our appointment schedule and remembered you from…"

"Ya, ya. I remember. You're a good friend of Leana's, right?" Jonathon stumbled a little over his words as he realized Leana's name had never come up at their previous meeting. He quickly tried to interject something to distract her from his comment about Leana. "And we talked about the dance."

"Yes, I am. And yes, we did." She giggled a little as she slid a piece of paper and a pen under Jonathon's nose. "So, anyway, here is a little questionnaire that Mr. Ronello forgot to give you. It just asks you a few medical questions and what your goals are. You know… for working out. And I need the signed waiver from your parents."

Jonathon pulled the waiver from his pocket, suddenly feeling a little unnerved at how sloppily he was dressed and about giving personal information to Leana's best friend. Kendra would surely be relaying details of their meeting to Leana during their next girl-time. Glad that he didn't have any medical restriction or medications to report, he took the pen and began filling out the form, aware of her standing a few short feet away waiting.

"So, did you decide if you're going to the dance?" Kendra asked as he was still writing.

He looked up. "I might. If I survive this." He pointed at the closed door behind her that led to the gym. They both gave a short laugh. He finished filling out his goals and wrote *TO GET FIT AND BUILD MUSCLE.* Then he slid the paper back across the counter.

"OK. Go ahead and have a seat. Mr. Ronello will be out in a few minutes. I think he's actually the one who will be training you today. Scotty is out sick."

Jonathon assumed now that Mr. Ronello was, in fact, Jim, the owner. He went to have a seat on a corner bench. The lobby area décor had an industrial appeal, with polished, plank-style seating and fixtures of brass and nickel. He picked up a *Men's Fitness* magazine lying on an end table and began thumbing through it for something to do while he waited. A minute passed and he set the magazine down, trying to muster up the nerve to ask Kendra another question.

"So...are you guys going to the dance? *Please don't tell Leana I asked,* he thought.

Kendra looked to be texting on her phone and glanced up. "I think so. Leana is coming by here in a little bit. I haven't seen her much this week. But we talked about it last week, so...ya, probably."

Jonathon felt himself starting to sweat at the thought of Leana walking in the door. "Will Jim be out soon?" he asked as he stood and began to pace, watching out the window to the street.

Just then, Jim came walking through the door behind her. "Hello, my man." He sashayed around the counter and grabbed Jonathon's hand, shaking it with such enthusiasm, Jonathon wasn't sure his arm would stay in his shoulder socket. "Are you ready?"

Jonathon pulled back quickly and fought the urge to massage the arm Jim had nearly dislocated. Without hesitancy, Jonathon said he couldn't wait to get started and brushed past Jim to lead the way through the gym entrance.

"Hah! I like your eagerness!" Jim slapped him on his back as he followed. "But we're gonna need you to get some better shoes for next time, ya hear?"

As Jonathon opened the back door to enter, he looked down at his feet. He was wearing Topsiders and realized he should have worn his court shoes. "Those don't have any support, my son. You need some running shoes."

With that, Jonathon scurried into the gym, hoping to avoid Leana and praying that Kendra wouldn't bring her to the back for any reason.

The air-conditioned gymnasium felt good on Jonathon's clammy skin. Jim took him into the locker room to store his backpack but told him to keep his water bottle handy as he gave a husky laugh. He noticed there were several guys over in the free weight section who seemed to know one another and felt glad when Jim led him in a different direction to begin instruction on use of the machines.

Jim thoughtfully set the weight of the first machine to a position unlikely to cause Jonathon any embarrassment. As he was beginning the first set of reps, a loud holler came from across the gym.

"HEY, JON!" Bryan Corwin was frantically waving. "What are YOU doing here?" A few of Bryan's group turned to eye Jonathon and Jonathon looked up at Jim who was giving him a big smile.

"You know this guy?" Jim laughed.

Jonathon finished the set of reps before answering Jim. "He's a guy on my debate team." Then he gave Bryan a nonchalant wave as he moved to the next machine, not answering his question.

Jim began to laugh more. "That explains it. No wonder he argues about everything." He turned around and hollered back to Bryan and repeated himself. "No wonder you argue about everything!" Then he turned back to face Jonathon. "I thought baseball was all that guy knew. Debate team, huh?"

A lump started to form in Jonathon's throat. "Is that the baseball team?"

"Sure is," Jim answered as he began fidgeting with the weight adjustment on machine number two.

Some of the equipment blocked Jonathon's view of a few players but he scanned those he could see. Right smack dab in the middle stood JR. Jonathon couldn't believe how unlucky this day was turning out. Not only was Leana expected to come by to see her friend at the desk but now he also had to run into his nemesis. He glanced back over toward the group, noticing their size. All had broad shoulders with biceps twice the size of his own. They were wearing razor back tanks with Cascadia logos and of course, proper shoes. He suddenly felt incredibly wimpy and uncomfortable.

"Okay, Jon. Step on over here and have a seat." Jim motioned for Jonathon to sit on the bench of yet another machine. Pretending he didn't notice JR and the entire team now watching him, he obeyed.

The remainder of the 30-minute intro session seemed to last forever, and Jonathon doubted he would remember a thing Jim had just shown him. He felt too distracted, thinking about his audience. He heard occasional bursts of laughter, which he hoped was not at his expense. Gradually, the team seemed to forget Jonathon was even there. By the time his session ended, Jonathon couldn't be happier to get going. He thanked Jim and felt grateful when he handed him a printout of everything they'd gone over. Unfortunately, Bryan and JR looked to have also finished their workouts and were heading toward the same exit door.

As they all neared each other, Bryan was overzealous about chatting it up with Jonathan. "Hey! Good to see you here!" He came up to him and wrapped one arm around a shoulder, giving him a big squeeze. JR had slowed his exit to politely acknowledge Jonathon.

"Hey," Jonathon greeted him timidly.

"How ya doin? JR replied.

Jonathon shook off Bryan's arm and gave a chuckle as he addressed them both. "Just joined and..." he nodded toward Jim in the distance. "...he, um, had to show me how some of these things work." Conscientious of his smaller stature while standing between the two athletes, Jonathon straightened his posture.

"You're Kate's friend, right?" JR threw in the unanticipated question, causing Jonathon to stammer for a second.

"Um, ya. I'm Kate's friend," Jonathon nodded, feeling proud to acknowledge this fact.

"We've spent a lot of time together recently. She talks about you a lot," JR huffed, emphasizing the last part.

Jonathon wasn't sure how he felt about that statement. *Did he mean she talked about him because they had been friends for so long? How much time had Kate been spending with this guy anyway?* He looked at the big guy's neck and could see a little evidence of the mark he'd noticed the night before. It looked to Jonathon like JR had applied makeup or something to conceal it. Some guy Jonathon had never seen before walked by and started chatting to Bryan, leaving Jonathon and JR standing quietly waiting.

Trying to fill the awkward silence, Jonathon spouted out, "We go way back. To like…first grade. She's a great girl." As he said it, melancholy rushed over him as he smiled thinking back on their first meeting in the lunch line at age six.

JR returned the grin. "I think so, too."

For some reason, Jonathon felt oddly irritated by JR's comment, and he made an excuse to leave. "I need to run. I'll probably see you guys around here again." He started to open the door when he caught a glimpse of Leana standing in the lobby talking to Kendra. The last thing he wanted was for her to see him sweaty, smelly and completely exhausted. He quickly closed the door in a panic. He looked around and breathed a sigh of relief when he realized he'd forgotten his backpack in a locker. "Geez, forgot my stuff. See ya, guys." He ran back toward the locker room, eyeing a side exit off the gymnasium where he could escape.

Jonathon took a roundabout route to stop into Grocer's Corner on the way home. By now, he was wishing he had driven; his legs already heavy from the squats and weights Jim had included in their first session. Although the day was warm and sunny, Jonathon wished he had time to go collapse on his bed. His anticipation for the rest of the evening was the only thing keeping his adrenaline surging so he could remain focused.

By the time he got to the front of the market his head was twirling with the possibility of seeing Leana and hopefully carrying out his plan successfully. He wasn't sure if his newest plan would work, but he definitely couldn't stand by and do nothing. Pulling out his phone, he did a search on prunes and their effect on the digestive system. Looking for other details, like how many prunes one could eat without causing harm to someone, and how long after eating them does it take to get results, he took screenshots of the information for later reference. All he was looking to do tonight was detain Jasper a little.

Once inside, Jonathon stopped to look around. He seldom shopped for himself and felt somewhat lost. Once he found the produce section, he watched others hand-picking their fruits and vegetables, inspecting and weighing them before bagging. He felt too embarrassed to ask for help finding prunes, so he grabbed a produce bag and began weaving between neatly organized rows of organic tomatoes, avocadoes and lettuce. *I had no idea there are so many kinds of apples*, he pondered as he strolled past the various signs for *RED DELICIOUS, FUJI, GALA* and more. He stopped in front of the refrigeration section displaying a host of nicely manicured vegetables. *I do NOT want to ask someone where to find prunes!* he thought, contemplating his options. He turned to take another stroll through and sighed a breath of relief as he stood staring straight at a bin with a large hand-drawn sign reading *PLUMS*. Remembering prunes were simply dried plums, he opened the plastic bag and shoved in a dozen, quickly leaving the area as soon as he could, not caring about their appearance or weight. Next, he searched for prune juice. After hunting for several minutes, he began feeling frustrated. Working up the courage, he humbly walked up to a worker who was stocking shelves.

"Excuse me, but can you please tell me where I can find prune juice?" Barely finishing his question, Jonathon noticed the middle-aged man looking at the bag of plums he was holding. The worker gave Jonathon a wry smile as Jonathon felt his face beginning to heat up.

"Sure, buddy." He chuckled quietly as he turned to point toward the back of the store. "Back on aisle 3 near the other fruit juices. Look on the bottom shelf." He then turned back toward Jonathon. "Hope it's not for you my friend. You're too young to need that stuff. My dad…he's…" The worker cocked his head and looked around. When he came up with his father's age, he continued. "… eighty-eight years old. He drinks it all of the time, you know, so he doesn't get blocked up." The man chuckled but Jonathon's bewildered stare back at the worker let him know this was too much information. Clearing his throat, the worker apologized. "Sorry… um, you can buy prunes pitted in a package, you know. It's easier than drinking the juice…or eating all those." He pointed to the bag in Jonathon's hand. "Trust me. They're hanging back by the bin where you found those."

Feeling a bit embarrassed, Jonathon lied, saying they were for his grandfather and thanked the employee. He sashayed through the aisles, back to the produce section. Sure enough, right next to the bin on a small shelf sat several brands of packaged prunes. He looked around and when he felt no one was watching, dumped all of the plums back into the bin and grabbed the cheapest bag of pre-pitted prunes.

He then made his way back through the store to finally locate the juice. Discovering that small cans only came in a six-pack, he settled on a quart-sized bottle.

Then he went to the freezer section to select a half gallon of vanilla ice cream. As he was shutting the glass door to the freezer case, Jonathon froze, though, not from the cold. Leana and Kendra had just rounded the corner at the other end of the aisle. Luckily, they were deep in discussion and seemed to not notice Jonathon.

Panicked, he quickly turned his back to them and headed the other direction at a frantic pace toward the back of the store. He power-walked the outer perimeter, making his way slowly toward the front registers. Stopping to peer down each aisle he passed, he made sure the girls weren't also heading toward the exit. His hands were sweating profusely as he struggled carrying the bag of prunes, the large bottle of juice and the ice cream carton, which was now turning slimy beneath his clammy fingers. The frost on the outside was beginning to melt and he could feel it sliding from his grip. *What kind of luck do I have that these two were only a few minutes behind me and happened to come to the store at the exact same time!* He pondered the irony in his mind. He hadn't wanted Leana to see him sweaty in his gym clothes, but now he ESPECIALLY did not want her to see him with this particular armful of groceries! Once the coast seemed clear, he dashed to the only checkout with no line and quickly paid for the items before running out the door.

When Jonathon arrived home, he felt relieved he hadn't run into anyone else he knew. His ice cream was already turning to mush and would not have survived another delay. He entered through the side garage door, so he could hide the ammunition in the spare garage refrigerator/freezer his family reserved for storing extra beverages and food. He shoved the juice and prunes toward the back and rearranged some sparkling water bottles in front to hide them. Doubting anyone would be looking in the freezer, but just to be sure, he hid the ice cream toward the back behind some frozen vegetable packages.

When he went inside, he hoped to slip upstairs unnoticed. But as the door clicked shut, he heard Lulu calling from the kitchen. "Is that you, Mrs. Samuels?"

Jonathon poked his head inside the kitchen door. "Just me, Lulu." She stood looking at him with a frown on her face and rollers in her hair.

"Why you coming in that way? You never come in that way."

Jonathon stuttered a second while trying to collect his thoughts for an excuse. "I… I just needed to put some ice cream in the freezer. It was starting to melt."

"You bought ice cream?" Lulu eyed Jonathon suspiciously. "You know I'll always add it to my shopping list when you want me to."

"I know, Lulu. I just worked out at the gym and..." Her eyebrows raised and her signature hand to the hip warned Jonathon that she wasn't quite buying his story. "…and I just got in the mood for a shake…so I stopped and bought some. No big deal, Lulu." He threw his hands up in the air for emphasis before letting the door swing shut.

"OK. You want me to make you your shake?" Lulu called out from behind the door.

Jonathon stopped on the stairs and shouted back down to make sure she heard him correctly. "No, Lulu." I want to get cleaned up first. Please don't! I will just make it when I'm ready." He waited a few seconds to make sure there was no rebuttal before rushing up to his room.

Jonathon decided a long, hot shower would feel good on his muscles that were already beginning to feel tense from the workout. Just before getting in, he noticed he had a text from Leana.

Sorry Jon! Yes. Your notes were very helpful 🥰 Kendra said you were at the gym today... I was going to thank you in person but you were already gone. See you at the dance!

As Jonathon let the pulsating shower hit his back, he closed his eyes and smiled thinking of that last line. He was starting to feel confident his plan might work. Just to be sure, as soon as he stepped out of the shower, he grabbed his phone and sent a text to Jasper to confirm he'd be stopping by in a couple of hours. Jasper quickly replied with a thumbs-up. With that, Jonathon wrapped the bath towel around his waist and sat down at his desk. "Okay, REMY." Jonathon patted the side of the machine as if it was a beloved pet. He then pulled out the attached keyboard to get down to business. "Time to work your magic for ME tonight instead of everyone else!" he murmured. Although serious, he couldn't help but laugh out loud as he thought of the other stored dreams he had in his Machine that had seemed to work perfectly on his dad, Lulu and Jasper. He began inputting a dream about himself, one intended for Leana. If everything went as planned, tonight was the night that would change everything for him.

After he programmed the dream for Leana, Jonathon tried to work on some homework, but the workout and warm shower had sent his body into a submissive calm. The last thing he remembered as he now woke up with a jolt was lying down to relax for only a minute. He grabbed his phone to look at the time. It was already after 4:00 p.m.!

Still wearing only his towel, Jonathon rushed to his closet and stood staring at his wardrobe for an appropriate outfit for the dance. Hoping he guessed correctly, he threw on a pair of designer jeans his mom had purchased for him at the beginning of the year and a burgundy light weight V-neck sweater. He wasn't sure if he should wear dress shoes. It was just a dance in the gym after all. Over the years, he had heard Kate asking her friends what they were wearing to this place and that, but he certainly wasn't going to text Jasper to ask him what HE was planning to wear. He decided on a pair of brown leather sneakers. *Nice but not too casual,* he thought. Then he began tidying up his room. Thinking that a candle might add a nice effect for later, he slipped down the hall toward his parents' bedroom to borrow one. Their door was ordinarily open at this time of day, however, this afternoon it was closed. He could hear his mom's undecipherable voice followed by his father's laughter from within. Jonathon rolled his eyes even though he was inwardly comforted by their renewed attention to one another. *At least REMY worked well for them*, he thought, gloating. He diverted his plan and turned to tiptoe down the stairs.

Peeking through the kitchen door to find the coast clear of Lulu, he ran out to the garage freezer to collect the ice cream and then the prunes and juice. He hunted through a few cupboards looking for the blender. Unsuccessful, he softly closed the doors to avoid making any attention-worthy noise and leaned against the counter, frustrated. Before he had time to come up with an alternate plan, he looked down, noticing Lulu had left the blender sitting out in plain sight along with an ice cream scoop. He shook his head, smiling at her attentiveness. *I can always count on her to come through.*

He pulled out his phone and Googled prune smoothies. From what he was reading, the taste could be enhanced if he added another fruit. He opened the refrigerator, excited to find some blueberries left over from when Lulu made her muffins. "I sure hope she isn't planning on using these for pancakes tomorrow," he mumbled to himself.

He opened the bag of pitted prunes and dumped every one of them into the empty blender. Making sure the kitchen door was closed, he hit the pulsate button in short bursts to quickly grind them into smaller pieces. Jonathon cringed with each loud whirr of the machine. He worried someone would appear any minute to ask what all the racket was about. As soon as the prunes looked like mush, he turned it off and sat quietly, listening for potential footsteps. As he waited a moment, he contemplated if using the entire bag was a good idea. But quickly remembering his intent, he left them all in and began scooping in some vanilla ice cream with a handful of the berries and a little prune juice. He unplugged the blender and carried it out to the garage, being careful to close the door behind him without letting it slam. He plugged it into the outlet on the workbench and turned it on, letting his concoction churn away until he seemed to have the consistency of a milkshake. He picked up the blender and eyed the mixture through the glass. The blueberries hadn't quite been able to mask the brown color of the prunes and Jonathon worried it might not look visually appetizing to Jasper. He carried it back into the kitchen, still trying to be quiet, grabbing a long teaspoon to sample the drink. Jonathon sipped at the spoon and felt pleasantly surprised by its refreshing taste. *It's different,* he thought, *yet I wouldn't mind having a little more.* Knowing the effect of the prunes, he decided the small taste was more than enough. He threw a couple more whole blueberries into the mixture for aesthetic appeal.

High up on a shelf above the regularly used glasses, he found a collection of large plastic cups with lids, many displaying team logos and other marketing prints that were likely giveaways from corporate events. He retrieved one that had a lid and straw and filled it to the brim. Then he walked it out to the garage freezer to keep it from melting while he cleaned up.

He was just drying the cannister portion of the blender when he heard someone coming into the kitchen behind him. He jumped a little even though he had disposed of all the prune packaging and juice bottle by shoving them to the bottom of the trash container.

"Oh! Lulu! You scared me!" Jonathon yelled as he spotted her out of the corner of his eye. Then turning to face her, he gasped slightly. She looked beautiful. Her dark silky hair normally worn in a bun atop her head was flowing in soft curls to just below her shoulders. She had on a magenta-colored knee length dress and a pair of high heels adorned with small tropical flowers complimenting the dress. A small white flower clip held her hair back on one side.

"Scared you?" She spotted the glass jar of the blender in his hand. "Why? Because I caught you making your own shake!" she snickered, eyeing him suspiciously.

Jonathon gathered himself. "Oh." He held up the evidence. "Yes. Caught red-handed! Lulu, you look beautiful!" he blurted out.

Lulu uncharacteristically became speechless, and though Jonathon felt it was impossible to tell, she seemed to be blushing.

"I mean…you just…you don't usually, you know…" He waved his hand up and down as if he was presenting an auction item.

Lulu fanned his hands away and giggled. "I'm going to a dance, remember?"

Jonathon did remember although it hadn't been in the forefront of his mind.

"I'm going to chaperone you!" she teased.

"Well, you can chaperone all you want. But there'll be lots of others there that probably need it more than me." Jonathon turned to finish cleaning up.

Lulu frowned. "Things not going well with Miss Leana?" she asked.

"Not really." Jonathon continued his task and mumbled under his breath just barely loud enough for Lulu to hear.

Sensing it was a sore subject, she decided to not pry. "Where's that shake? Do you have any leftovers?"

Jonathon gulped before replying. "I drank it. It's all gone. Hope you don't mind that I used most of the blueberries that were in the fridge."

"No problem. I just need a few in the morning. You look pretty dapper too, Jon-Jon." She winked with a grin. "Are you heading out now? It's a bit early. Aren't you going to have any dinner? I made some…"

Jonathon put up his hand to stop her. "Thanks, Lulu. That milkshake filled me up. I'm okay. I'm heading over to Jasper's before the dance."

"AH! I was wondering what happened between you two. He's barely been around in the past couple of weeks."

Jonathon grimaced, thinking of the reasons his friend hadn't been around. "It's all good," he lied. "I was wondering what mom and dad are doing home on a Saturday… together?" He threw a glance upward in the direction of their room.

Lulu went to the refrigerator and pulled out a few slices of cheese. "I suspect it's none of our business. But it's good." She gave

Jonathon another wink. "I'm going to go finish getting ready. I'll see you at the dance?"

Jonathon turned to Lulu before she exited. "Can I ask you something, Lulu?"

She stopped and fanned her hands out in question. "Shoot."

"What did you actually dream about that caused you to…you know…pursue Mr. Mercado?"

Lulu raised her eyebrows. "Well…there's no harm in you asking." She paused and brought her finger to the side of her mouth.

Jonathon held his breath, thinking he was about to hear the climax of a great story.

"But…that doesn't mean I'm going to tell you," she laughed. Then twirling around, she left the kitchen, fanning her face.

***

Jonathon had placed the milkshake container in a used plastic bag from the grocery store to carry it to Jasper's. Although the sun was lowering, the temperature outside was still quite warm. Afraid the milkshake would melt before he got to Jasper's, he picked up the pace, soon regretting wearing the sweater top.

As he approached the corner of Jasper's street, he slowed down to text his friend, asking him to come out front. By the time Jonathon arrived, Jasper was sitting on his front porch. A giant sycamore tree engulfed his tiny front yard but provided a nice shade to the area. Jonathon slowed his approach as he neared the end of the walkway as Jasper leaned back against the top step with his elbows supporting him, cocking his head as he watched Jonathon.

"Hey, hey. buddy. I knew you couldn't stay mad at me forever." Jasper, always the clown, was trying to get his best friend to smile but Jonathon simply reached into the bag and pulled out the drink.

Jonathon shoved the smoothie toward Jasper, giving no expression. "A peace offering."

Jasper sat up and suspiciously reached for the drink. "What is it?"

"A date and berry smoothie. I made myself one and had leftovers." Jonathon stood nervously rocking on his heels as he crumpled up the plastic bag and waited for Jasper to take a taste." *Come on! Please like it,* he thought.

Jasper lifted the lid slightly and Jonathon stiffened with anticipation, afraid Jasper was going to take a close look at what was inside. Instead, Jasper simply sniffed it and put the lid back on. He took a long, labored sip through the straw. "It's thick, but pretty good. Since when do you make shakes? I bet Lulu made it…huh?" He raised the straw again to his lips and continued drinking.

Jonathon finally exhaled a giant sigh of relief once he felt sure Jasper was indeed enjoying the smoothie. "So, what did you have to tell me?"

Jasper squinted as a breeze moved the tree branches and let sunlight hit him smack in the face. He shielded his eyes with his free hand as he looked straight at Jonathon. "I know this whole thing didn't turn out like you wanted. And I didn't ask for it." He was talking rapidly, seeming worried he wouldn't be able to say everything he wanted before Jonathon interrupted. But Jonathon just sat back and let Jasper continue.

"I...well, we...really like each other. And I just can't help it, Jon. I want you to understand. You ***know*** me. I haven't ever really had a real girlfriend. But with Leana, it's different. She is so easy to talk to. I just want to be with her all of the time."

He stopped for a moment, waiting to see if Jonathon was ready to interject. When Jonathon simply crossed his arms and continued staring at his friend expressionless, Jasper felt the needed to continue. "You're my best friend. For how many years now? I don't want anything to change between us."

At that moment, Jonathon fought the urge to tell Jasper it was too late. "Whatever," he muttered sarcastically. "I said this is a peace offering. I can't change what's happened. I'll figure it out."

Jasper looked relieved but Jonathon stood there thinking about the word Jasper had used a moment before. *Girlfriend. Have he and Leana become* ***that*** *close in just under two weeks? Does Leana feel the same?* He pondered these questions just long enough to have a wave of self-doubt pour over him. Shaking his head to rid himself of any hesitancy, he pushed forward on his plan.

"Hey. Can I borrow your phone? Mine just died," Jonathon felt a weight of guilt as he lied.

Jasper reached in his back pocket. "Of course, dude."

Once Jasper put in his password and handed it off, Jonathon excused himself and turned to walk toward the giant tree to pretend he was making a call. Glancing over his shoulder, he noticed Jasper again sitting on the porch, powering down the shake. He had his eyes closed and was leaning back, letting what was left of the setting sun soak his face while humming some undecipherable tune.

Jonathon turned his back to him again and went to Jasper's contacts. He found Leana's name and with a swipe, deleted her info. Then he went to Jasper's messages. Jonathon noticed quite a long trail of texts between Jasper and Leana but didn't have the time to read them, nor did he want to. However, he did notice the last line. **Can't wait to see you** was followed by three heart emojis.

Jonathon felt sick to his stomach. Desperate, he quickly swiped to delete the entire line of texts, immediately cringing with remorse, knowing what he was doing was a terrible violation. He glanced over his shoulder again. Jasper was still very invested in his smoothie and not paying attention to Jonathon, so Jonathon quickly pulled his own phone from his pocket to view Leana's number. He paused and took a deep breath. Before he could change his mind, he went to the settings in Jasper's phone, typed in her number and put a block on it.

Realizing that a call or text from his own phone at that moment might reveal his deceit, Jonathon flipped his toggle to vibrate mode. Then, so Jasper would see he had made a call, he placed a call with Jasper's phone to his home's landline, knowing no one ever answered it. He hung up once the answering machine came on but pretended he was leaving a message.

Jonathon walked back to the porch and tossed the phone to Jasper. "Stand up a second." He gave a grin to Jasper, so he would oblige and even put his hand out to help him to his feet.

"Just one more thing I think I owe you." Jonathon tried to act like he was going in for a hug. Jasper took a step closer, but Jonathon stopped. "Hold still. You have a bug on your neck!" He quickly pretended to reach for a bug but instead pinched and twisted the skin just hard enough to hopefully cause a small bruise that would resemble a hickey like the one JR had.

Jasper let out a mournful sounding yelp as he flinched backwards. "What the…?"

He began massaging the side of his neck. "What was that about?! There was no bug!"

"I owed you SOMETHING for stealing the girl that I worked tirelessly to build a friggin machine for..." The look coming from Jasper made Jonathon feel horrible. Still, he hoped to leave a mark evident enough to show up on Jasper's dark skin.

"Whatever, dude. I gotta go inside!" He turned to go up the steps but yelled back over at Jonathon who had taken a couple of steps backwards as he watched him. "I hope that little stunt helped you get over it!" He was still holding his neck and shaking his head in disbelief as he entered the house.

The last thing Jonathon noticed as the screen door was slamming behind him was Jasper sucking down the last of his smoothie.

After leaving Jasper's, Jonathon walked the street at a slow pace. It wasn't quite time to go to the dance, and feeling his stomach grumbling, he began to realize he hadn't eaten anything since breakfast. Heading in the general direction of the school, he chose a short detour to swing by a local Ma & Pa restaurant to grab a bite to eat. The diner was one of his mom's favorite eateries, so Jonathon was very familiar with the farm-to-table menu. Sitting down in a corner booth where he had a nice view out the front window, he skimmed the menu for specials and quickly ordered once the waitress came by.

While waiting for his food to arrive, he pulled his phone out to play a game he had downloaded weeks before. He barely started playing when he set the phone down on the table, unable to concentrate. His mind was swirling with scenarios of how this evening might play out. When his chicken tacos with homemade chips and salsa arrived, he suddenly felt a little nauseous, making it difficult to eat. He sat picking at the meal while watching several students out the window beginning to make their way toward the school. He noticed Sarah Jonday from his debate team walking hand in hand with some guy who was miraculously taller than her. Most of the other students Jonathon did not recognize.

Once he was done picking at his food, he put his credit card in the holder left at the table's edge. The waitress came over with a concerned look on her face. He'd eaten less than half of his meal and Jonathon felt the need to make an excuse, stating simply that his eyes were bigger than his stomach. Then leaving a nice tip, he ducked out.

The evening air was getting cooler and as Jonathon left for the school, he was now happy to be wearing a sweater after all. He made another quick stop at a convenience store along the way to grab some mints. When he went to pay, he pulled his phone out of his pocket. He had missed a call from Leana. That was when he realized he had forgotten to unmute his ringer after leaving Jasper's house.

His heart started to race, wondering why she would be calling. She had never called before, only texted a few times. He stepped outside and hit her name for the return call and began pacing on the sidewalk in front of the store as he heard the phone ringing on the other end. The nausea he felt earlier was now replaced with knots in his stomach as he worried she was calling to say she was staying home tonight. *But why would she tell me if she changed her mind about going to the dance?*

"Hi, Jon." Leana's voice sounded rushed and concerned.

Jonathon tried to come off as calm as he could. "Hey, Leana. You still heading to the dance tonight?" He rolled his eyes at his own ridiculous question.

"Um. Ya. But I was wondering...have you talked to Jasper today?"

Jonathon grimaced at her concern for Jasper. He took a giant gulp, cautiously thinking out his response. "Yes. I saw him just a little while ago. He had a bit of a stomach ache." He cringed with guilt as he blurted out the words.

"Oh. Well, I hope he's okay. I've been trying to reach him, but he hasn't responded. I guess I'll just see him tonight. It wasn't like him to not call me back." Her voice trailed off a bit as he sensed her shyness about revealing the closeness between her and Jasper.

Jonathon felt like a jerk lying to her but feeling it necessary to carry out his plan, he continued anyway. "Oh. He said he would be a little late getting to the dance. He mentioned his phone was acting up." He winced, feeling a mountain of shame piling on his shoulders with every sentence. Then, feeling too far in to turn back, he slapped his final hand on the table. "But, if he's late, I'll be happy to dance with you until he shows up." He bit his lip waiting for her answer, hoping she wouldn't blow him off.

"Ah. That's so sweet of you. Maybe I'll take you up on that." She then thanked him and told him she'd see him in a bit. As he hung up, perspiration seemed to be coming out of every pore in his body. And the sweater he wore was again, too warm.

Jonathon reached the campus outside the gymnasium, finding a few booths scattered on the lawn for couples or groups of friends to dress up in hats and glasses to have their picture taken. A giant wooden arch adorned in various flowers and ivy had been placed in front of the entrance doors to the gym, providing a hint of ambiance before entering. On a giant hand painted sign, colorful, well-scripted letters read *WELCOME TO CASCADIA GARDEN PARTY.* Members of the student council stood at the door selling tickets to those who hadn't pre-purchased as well as raffle tickets for a "surprise door prize." The guys who were working were wearing leafy wreaths on their heads, while the girls donned floral crowns. Music from within blared loud enough to be heard a block away with a heavy beat that resonated under the skin of anyone within 50 feet.

Jonathon easily spotted Mia who towered over the group at the entrance. She was genuinely acknowledging every single student making their way inside. A handful of teachers gathered a few yards from the front doors. Jonathon assumed they were chaperones but he saw no sign of Mr. Mercado and Lulu. Several groups of students were congregated on the lawn not seeming overly anxious to enter. Feeling out of place standing by himself, Jonathon searched for anyone he knew well enough to join and for a brief second, he wished Jasper was with him. Then he began to wonder when Kate would arrive, or if she might already be inside.

In the distance, he noticed a few people he was acquainted with from his English class but no one he really wanted to join. Jonathon pulled out his phone to text Kate but quickly put it back in his pocket when he eyed JR and some of his teammates walking up the sidewalk toward the school. For some reason, the sight of JR made Jonathon suddenly feel as if weights were sitting on his chest. He drew in a deep breath to shake the feeling and glanced in JR's direction looking for Kate, relieved she wasn't with the group. *Why do I even care*? he thought. He noticed the group stop out by the street. They seemed to be giving farewells to each other. Then JR jogged across the street in a different direction, back toward the main part of town.

Relieved by JR's exit, Jonathon wondered why he felt such distress around the guy and thought it likely because he had been his competition for Leana's feelings. Or maybe he worried this jock may be playing with Kate's feelings. Jonathon felt some level of protectiveness over his longtime friend. Before turning to go inside, it occurred to him that maybe JR was heading out to retrieve Kate as his date and another thought crossed his mind. *What if Kate was the one who gave JR the hickey?* Several feelings began to stir inside of him, including nausea. Whatever the reason, Jonathon was glad JR left the school.

Determined to remain focused, Jonathon tried to clear his mind. He needed to find Leana before Jasper arrived and continued eyeing the grounds for any remote friendships as he made his way to the front of the gym and bought a ticket for the dance.

The gymnasium was darkened with twinkling lights strung strategically across the ceiling to look like stars high overhead. A giant neon light shaped like a crescent moon hung above the dance floor near the distant wall. Hundreds of plants and trees surrounded the interior of the gym, while others were randomly scattered throughout, giving the feel of a stylish city park. Amongst the trees sat bistro tables with added chairs for seating. The floor looked to be protected by brown packing paper with bark scattered on it for an outdoor effect. The committee had used cafeteria benches to resemble park benches in a few spots along a taped-off path leading toward the dance floor. The final props were a few rented streetlamps, one placed next to each park bench.

The scene was absolutely jaw-dropping and Jonathon stood in awe of the efforts Mia's committee had made for this school dance. As he stood just inside the door gawking at the gym's transformation, a familiar voice startled him.

"Looks amazing, doesn't it?" Kendra Lake was standing at his side with her arms locked behind her back, looking around the room. "So, you decided to come." It came off as more of a statement than a question as she was practically yelling just to be heard over the pounding beat of the music.

"Hey." Jonathon shouted back nervously as he took a quick scan of the gym, hoping to find Leana. "I…am speechless!" he replied. "I can't believe the school spends so much for…a dance."

Kendra chuckled. "Well, do you know Bo Sampson?"

"Who?" Jonathon could barely hear himself think.

"Bo Sampson," Kendra pronounced each syllable as loud and deliberately as she could.

Jonathon shook his head no. He had never even heard his name.

"Well, his dad owns the Plant Palace." She was now leaning in and speaking toward Jonathon's ear. "He is LOANING us these plants." She drew out the word loaning with a heavy emphasis. "As long as they all get back to him in good condition, we don't have to worry. Bo and his buddies even delivered them." She gave a smile and raised her eyebrows to Jonathon as if to gesture an amazing feat. "Almost everything else except for the rented lampposts and that moon." She pointed in the direction of the giant hanging light. "...everything else is stuff from here at school."

Jonathon again shook his head in amazement. "Glad I came." He turned to Kendra. He took a deep breath trying to get the nerve to ask if Leana was there yet. He didn't want to act so obvious and have Kendra tell her he was asking about her. He leaned down so she could hear him without him shouting. "Did you come alone?" As soon as Jonathon spit out those words, he recognized they may have come across differently than intended. "I mean...are you just working this event?" He felt his face flushing and was glad the gym was relatively dark.

"Oh, we got here early to help Mia with last-minute decorating. Leana and me. She's somewhere, probably looking for your friend Jasper." She rolled her eyes and gave a twisted turn of her lip. Her comment made Jonathon stand up straight and take a deep breath. Just then, Kendra grabbed one of Jonathon's arms, startling him. "Oh shoot. I forgot...I gotta go find Mia. Talk to you later, Jon!"

Kendra ran back out the door, so Jonathon turned to begin walking the mock path, looking around for any sight of Leana. Back in a far corner near an exit door, he then spotted Lulu and Mr. Mercado. His teacher looked to be introducing Lulu to another teacher. Jonathon hoped Lulu would mind her own business tonight and stick to chaperoning.

Walking at a snail's pace, Jonathon felt the music was annoyingly loud as he approached the still empty dance floor. He was happy to see a four-person band in a back corner setting up and tuning their guitars. He hoped they wouldn't be as loud as what was playing over the intercom. He continued walking between a cluster of trees and found a small table for three and pulled out a seat. Lowering himself onto the chair, he felt sore from his workout earlier in the day and he let out a long, drawn-out groan until he got situated. The gymnasium was beginning to fill up with students now, so Jonathon leaned back to people-watch. That was when he finally spotted Leana across the room. Relief poured over him and a huge smile swept across his face. She was explaining something to a small cluster of girls. As he pondered going over to interrupt, Kate's head poked out from behind the tallest girl in the circle. She was staring straight at Jonathon.

She gave a little wave and a smile and then lifted her phone towards him and pointed at it. Jonathon frowned at first, not understanding what she was saying but then realized she wanted him to look at his phone. He reached into his pocket and pulled it out. There was a message from Kate 38 minutes ago, and one from Jasper within five minutes. He opened Kate's first.

Hey you. If you really do show up tonight, can I have the first dance? 👻

He looked across the room and gave her a thumbs-up. She then grinned and returned the gesture before turning around to continue chatting with her group. Then he opened Jasper's text.

> **DUDE! Either that shake or my lunch didn't sit well with me. Can you find Leana and tell her I'll be late? Something is up with my phone and I can't find her number!**

Jonathon simply replied, **Of Course,** while feeling the giddy anticipation of actually pulling off his plan. Knowing he needed to get busy before Jasper got there, Jonathon stood up to go get Kate. He felt an intense ache in each thigh as he tried to rise. His muscles were definitely starting to tighten up. He realized now that it was a stupid move to exercise for the first time before going to a dance.

With perfect timing, the song overhead ended and the lead singer of the band grabbed the microphone to welcome everyone. Applause and a few shouts erupted before he introduced himself and the band members who called themselves Between-The-Covers, and then joked that they were a cover-band. A few chuckles could be heard as the band began with a popular, slow, throwback song. "Just to get you warmed up!" Jack, the lead member, shouted before starting in on the lyrics.

Jonathon hobbled toward the group of girls when he spotted Leana and one other girl out of the corner of his eye. They were scurrying back toward the entrance like they were on a mission. He felt a pit in his stomach, worrying about whether she would return soon, but at the same time relieved to not have her there while he danced with Kate.

Sensing his presence, Kate turned around. Jonathon gave her a wink and held his hand out. "I believe this dance was reserved for me?"

Jonathon wasn't expecting Kate to look so beautiful, but the twinkling reflection of the overhead lights made her hair glow and her eyes sparkle. Her usual straight hair had a soft curl at the ends and was pulled back off to one side with a clip. He wasn't sure but he thought she looked a bit different, and he wondered if she was wearing a little makeup. Kate noticed Jonathon intently looking at her. She lowered her head and held her hand over her mouth to suppress a bashful giggle.

"Let's see what all those years of cotillions did for you," she teased.

Jonathon snapped out of his gaze and took her hand, leading her to where several couples were already making their way onto the floor. He put one arm around her waist and held the other hand as he'd been taught. Most of the other couples dancing were closely embraced, some practically mauling each other. This made him feel awkward as he tried to keep a small distance between him and Kate. He suddenly wished that this first song would have been a fast one.

They stepped and rocked to the beat, Jonathon towering over her. The top of Kate's hair brushed along his chin as she leaned in a little and he picked up the subtle, pleasant citrusy scent of her perfume. They danced through half of the song without saying a thing to each other and Jonathon wondered why he was suddenly at a loss for words. To break the awkwardness, he tried to make conversation over the music that was still quite loud.

"So, were you helping out here tonight? I saw you with the girls that seem to be running the show."

Kate looked up at him with a concerned look on her face which puzzled him. "I worked on quite a few little things since I was here early." She looked back down at Jonathon's feet. "You're a pretty good dancer Jon, except…are you limping?"

Jonathon laughed. "You won't believe this but I joined a gym today. I can hardly walk now." He was joking but when it came down to it, he wondered if by the end of the night he might truly need a wheelchair.

"Wow. Good for you!" And with that comment she gently rested her head on his shoulder. Jonathon suddenly became uncomfortable. He had always felt such ease around his friend but nerves were beginning to take over and he pushed back just a little.

Kate stopped dancing and looked up at him. She had a hurt look on her face as she peered into his eyes and dropped both of her hands. "I need to go."

Jonathon instantly felt responsible for her wanting to leave, though he thought her reaction to him stepping back was rather extreme. "Why? I…" he knew he didn't want her to leave because of him. "…I didn't mean anything and the song's not over. Let's finish…" he stuttered.

She shook her head. "It's okay. I gotta go. JR is expecting me later."

He felt guilty for ruining the whole evening for her on the very first dance. "Kate… seriously? You haven't even been here that long." It was too dark to know for sure but he thought her eyes looked glassy as if she were about to cry. Then he wondered why JR hadn't come to the dance with her if she was so anxious to go meet him.

"I've actually been here for several hours. I hope you have a fun night, Jon." She leaned forward onto her tiptoes and gave him a very tight hug that seemed to him lasted longer than a typical goodbye hug. Then she turned and sprinted off the dance floor without looking up. Luckily, he didn't feel stranded on the dance floor for long as the song was just ending, so he joined the other students walking back to their prospective places.

Jonathon had a momentary urge to follow Kate and ask what was going on with her. But since she was headed to meet JR, he thought, why bother? He had come to the dance with another agenda anyway. He surveyed the gymnasium looking for Leana as he walked back to his seat. When he got back to his table, he found a couple of female classmates who were deeply engrossed in conversation seated in the extra chairs, holding hands affectionately and looking to be on the verge of a kiss. They didn't even look up at Jonathon when he approached, so he decided to continue walking around.

He made his way back toward the entrance when he noticed Leana standing over by a lamppost looking around like she was searching for someone. Jonathon made his way through the groups of students to where she was standing. "Hi, Leana!" he shouted since he was afraid the music might drown him out.

Leana jumped and placed her hand over her heart, and then started laughing. "You scared me!" She continued looking around. "Do you know if Jasper is here yet?"

Jonathon was disappointed that a question about Jasper was what first spilled out of her beautiful full lips, but he was happy to provide an explanation for his disappearance. "He told me to tell you he wasn't feeling great and to keep you occupied until he could arrive."

"Oh reaaallly?" She seemed amused by his statement but then became concerned. "Is he okay?"

"Ya. It's just a little stomach bug or something, I think. You want to dance?"

Leana wrung her hands together nervously. "I will. But I warn you that I am not a good dancer." She gave Jonathon the big, beautiful smile that had originally attracted him to her. "Now?"

"Yes. Now is good. And you don't have to worry about how you dance. My legs are so sore from the gym I can hardly move them anyway." She chuckled and then he motioned his arm to wave her to go first.

On their way to the dance floor, Jonathon noticed Lulu still standing in the distant corner where she had been earlier, now watching him and Leana. She gave him her giant grin and raised her eyebrows like only she could and then started in on a little clapping motion. Jonathon turned quickly toward Leana, desperately hoping she didn't notice.

Luckily, Leana was eyeing the other dancers and hadn't noticed Lulu.

Just as they reached the dance floor, the band ended a slow song and began one that was more upbeat. The two of them stood there awkwardly at first and again laughed out loud, hiding any insecurities. They began dancing, neither one feeling very confident. Occasionally they exchanged glances, each time met with chuckles. Jonathon prayed for the next song to be a slow one. *Awful timing,* he thought. Cotillions had prepared him for ballroom and slow dances. Luckily, he did have some rhythm and, like most teenagers, had practiced dancing to the radio when he was home alone. But tonight, a combination of nerves and aching muscles made him feel like he was sinking in quicksand, not dancing. His feet felt like lead while he rocked his upper body and arms spastically. When the song ended and another fast song began, Jonathon quickly decided to offer to get Leana something to drink.

They reached the beverage table where a beautiful flow of pink punch spilled from a smaller bowl down into a large ornate basin. Next to the punch were rows and rows of bottled waters. A decorated sign read *Cascadia Fountain.* Jonathon filled a paper cup with punch and handed it to Leana.

"Thanks, Jon." She seemed anxious as she surveyed the room. "So what do you think?" She was trying to create a conversation.

"Of the dance?" he asked. She gave him a look that signaled it was obvious. "Of course," he nodded. "I think it's amazing! Looks like a ton of work went into it. Good job! You helped a lot, right?" He knew she had and was enjoying seeing the delight in her eyes with his acknowledgement.

"I was on a committee to help with…" Just then she stopped talking and her eyes widened as she was looking in the distance past Jonathon. He turned to see what had caught her eye. It was Jasper coming in the entrance.

Jonathon felt his hopes sink, annoyed by the bad timing of Jasper's arrival which was much earlier than he had planned. "Figures," Jonathon muttered. He didn't think Leana could hear his comment due to the pounding vibrations coming through the nearby speakers close by but she turned and looked at him oddly.

"What?" she frowned.

Jonathon bent over and grabbed his leg. "Sorry, it's my legs. They're just so sore," he half-lied.

Her attention left Jonathon as her smile widened when Jasper approached them. "Hey, you two! Have you been eating it up on the dance floor?" Jasper laughed, but eyed Jonathon suspiciously.

"Jonathon was nice enough to dance with me once." She giggled but then as if a switch flipped, her mood went from chipper to somber. Her mouth dropped a little and Jonathon noticed her staring straight at Jasper's neck. Jonathon held his breath, wishing he could read her mind. All evening he had worried that the pseudo-hickey he gave Jasper might not quite show up against his dark skin but it stood out even more than Jonathon thought possible.

"So, Jasper," Leana suddenly became very business-like. "What were you doing this afternoon that made you late for the dance?" Her question came off snarky and Jonathon could tell she was not at all pleased. He stood back with his arms crossed, inwardly gloating at being successful with this stage of his plan.

Instead of answering Leana, Jasper was holding his stomach with one hand and squirming in apparent discomfort. "I'm…" He doubled over for a second, then stood back up. "I'm sorry. I'll be right back." He took off running toward the bathroom.

Jonathon knew his friend was experiencing problems because of the prune shake, and he momentarily had to remind himself this was no time for guilt or pity. In fact, he felt Jasper somewhat deserved a little misery.

Leana was looking at the ground with a sad, scorned look. Her hands were even shaking a little. Feeling brief remorse for being responsible for her distress, Jonathon knew he needed to let those feelings go if his plan was to work. And he needed to act quickly before Jasper returned.

"I'm sorry. I can tell you're disappointed. Can you come with me to my house for a bit? I think Jasper will be busy for a while." This statement was likely true but for different reasons than what Jonathon was suggesting.

Leana looked straight into Jonathon's eyes with a look that scared him a little. "I absolutely will!" She then grabbed Jonathon's hand and headed toward the door. She stopped for a moment as they were exiting and dropped his hand. "Just a sec." She went over to Kendra and whispered something.

While he stood there waiting, Jonathon kept watch of the area where trees were providing privacy to the restroom doors. He was literally praying that Jasper would be busy inside for a while longer. Just then Kate's friend Tessa came walking up.

"Hi, Jon. Where are you heading?" She looked toward the door. "You leaving?" She paused for just a second when Jonathon looked agitated but then she asked, "…to go find Kate?"

"Huh? Find Kate?" Jonathon wondered what in the heck she meant by that and gave her a dumbfounded look.

Tessa twisted her mouth as if suggesting he was stupid. But then she flat out said it. "You guys. You can never see the writing on the wall, can you?" She turned around and walked off just as

Leana came back and again grabbed his hand to pull him out of the building.

The night air was cold but Jonathon was far from feeling the chill as he had to power walk just to keep up with Leana's determined pace. Each step was painful as his calves and shoulders had now joined the growing list of his aching muscles. Leana had let go of his hand when they first left the school campus and he trailed about a yard behind her since. Neither of them spoke the entire time. Jonathon was hoping she wouldn't ask why he wanted her to come over but at the same time he was a bit nervous about what *her* intentions were, since she had never even bothered to ask why.

Leana started to make a wrong turn when Jonathon directed her toward his street with a slight tug of her sleeve as he now took the lead. The moon was bright in the night sky, and even though they were a block and a half away from his house, he could see his dad's car parked in the driveway. Disappointment cascaded through his aching limbs. He had hoped his parents would be gone for the evening.

When they approached his house, Jonathon grabbed Leana's hand and led her through the back garage door, hoping the side entrance would allow them to slip upstairs unnoticed. There were no lights on in the living room but just to be safe, he turned to gesture for her to be quiet by raising a finger to his pursed mouth. She gave him a befuddled look and he realized it was because they still hadn't said a word to each other since leaving the dance. They quietly tiptoed up the stairs. He hadn't heard any voices from the kitchen and his parents' bedroom door was wide open to a darkened room. Happily, he assumed they had gone out after all.

Jonathon turned on his bedroom desk lamp for a more relaxed mood than the bright overhead light. Leana went straight for the bed and had a seat. Her previous visit had obviously helped her feel more comfortable in his room this time around.

"So," Leana spewed out. "What are we gonna do? How about that machine? I need to relax." Jonathon clumsily lowered himself onto his desk chair, holding on to the chair's arms. By now, his legs felt like Jell-O. Leana noticed his discomfort and couldn't stop a giggle. "You know…you need to go slow when you first start working out."

Although he was in pain, Jonathon was glad to hear something light-hearted coming out of her mouth. "Ya, well. I'll know better next time," he said with a subdued tone.

"I'm sorry. I didn't mean to…" She started to apologize.

"That's okay. I'm the one who thought I could show up the baseball team," Jonathon smiled. He felt unusually calm around her for a change and didn't mind casting himself as the fool.

She seemed to be relaxed now, too. "Kendra told me you were there for your first time. That's actually great."

Jonathon shook his head in acknowledgement. He turned toward REMY but didn't make a move to turn it on. Without looking at Leana, he asked, "You ready for me to hook you up? I mean…to the Machine." He felt his face heat up with his awkward wording.

Leana kicked her shoes off and lay back on the bed just as she had been instructed to do during her last visit. Not saying a word, he took that as a yes. Jonathon turned on his Machine and calmly began selecting the program he had entered; the one he hoped would give her a dream to make her feel about him the way Lulu now felt about Mr. Mercado. The way his father had revived his feelings for his mom. And…the way Jasper was now feeling about Leana.

With that last thought, Jonathon felt a pang in his gut. He had really done a number on his best friend. And now, he was on the brink of achieving his own personal goal to "get the girl." But he didn't feel good about it.

He slowly went through the motion of plugging in the earphones and acting like he was setting things up as he sat watching Leana. She was lying there looking like a princess from a fairytale. He looked back at his Machine and then hung his head briefly. He could feel his phone vibrating in his pocket, and he knew it was likely Jasper calling to give him a piece of his mind. He ignored it.

"Jon?" Leana sat up. When he looked up at her, he noticed she had tears running down her face. "What's wrong?" she asked.

Jonathon grabbed a tissue from the box on his nightstand and handed it to Leana. "Do you want to tell me why you are crying?"

Leana looked down as she blotted at her cheeks and eyes. "I really thought he liked me." She stopped for a second but then continued. “I mean, only me. I thought he was different than a lot of guys.” Then she started to cry harder. The tension had obviously built up on their walk and her emotions were breaking free.

Jonathon struggled to move his legs as he twisted to pivot the chair and reached for the whole box of tissues this time. He handed it to Leana. Then he rolled his desk chair closer to her and rubbed her back as she blew her nose between sniffles. “I think there’s a lot of things I can explain,” Jonathon whispered. Then he held his breath and cringed before asking her a question he didn’t necessarily want to know the answer to. “You really like him…a lot, don’t you?” She continued to cry softly and only nodded her head without looking up.

Jonathon struggled to stand up. “Put on your shoes. I have somewhere else I want to take you.” Keeping her head down, Leana did as she was told as he picked up his phone to type out a text.

Jonathon grabbed a jacket for himself and one of his sweaters to wrap around Leana before they left his room. As they walked down the quiet street back in the direction of the school, the wind was whipping and the streetlights casting graphic shadows of the oak trees lining the sidewalks created an eerie ambiance. He put his arm around her to offer her warmth, but for the first time in months, he felt nothing sensual. Only friendship and a desire to protect her.

As they made their way down the street, they heard dogs barking from every direction. "They're likely spooked by the wind," Jonathon said, referring to the dogs. Leana scrunched her shoulders while he tried to detect her mood. *What is she thinking?* Then as they rounded the corner in the direction of the school, the far-off boom-boom-boom of the bass echoed from the dance. "They're still going at it," Jonathon pointed out the obvious with a chuckle but Leana still remained quiet. At the next corner, he steered her in a different direction, down a street he knew well.

"Where are we going?" she asked, finally breaking her silence.

Jonathon contemplated telling her. He knew she was angry with Jasper and didn't want her to refuse seeing him. "All I can say is…what I am doing is trying to make up for something I did. I want my two friends to be happy."

Leana looked up at Jonathon with an amused look on her face but she didn't press him for more answers. When they approached Jasper's place, Jonathon stopped her at the sidewalk leading up to his house. "Wait here a minute." When she frowned, he added, "Please."

"This is Jasper's house. I don't even want to…" Leana's sentence was hushed by Jonathon when he put his finger to her lips.

"Maybe I don't deserve it, but please trust me. Okay?" Jonathon whispered.

She stared at him for a moment before slowly nodding her head and then stepped back, wrapping herself tighter in the sweater.

Jonathon walked slowly up the walkway and peered up at Jasper's window to see if a light was on. The shutters made it difficult to tell. He hoped Jasper was home by now. Pulling out his phone, he sent a follow-up text to the earlier one he'd sent when he and Leana were still at his house. He had asked Jasper to go home and told him he'd be by to explain everything.

Can you come down? Look out your window.

Not waiting for Jasper to answer, Jonathon put his phone back in his pocket and glanced out toward the street where Leana was quietly standing, looking wary. Then he looked up at Jasper's window and noticed the shutters now slightly open. Jasper was peering down at Leana on the sidewalk. A few seconds later, the front door swung open, and Jasper barreled out with a look of determination.

"You want to tell me what's going on?" he demanded. He brushed past Jonathon and stopped a few feet later, unsure of the situation. Jasper looked at Leana and then back at Jonathon. "Where in the hell did you take Leana?" He looked back at Leana whose face had uncertainty written all over it.

Jonathon calmly turned to call out Leana's name, motioning her to join them. Leana tightened the grip on her sweater, her arms rigid across her body. She paused before slowly approaching them. When she was nearer, they both noticed her bitter look of confusion and Jonathon put up his hands in front of each of them, signaling them to stay quiet while he spoke.

"Leana, I think you might have got the wrong impression about Jasper tonight." Leana started to say something, but Jonathon quickly jumped in to stop her. "I was angry at Jasper over..." he hesitated, "something, and..." This time Jasper started to chime in but Jonathon, also, abruptly stopped him from speaking. "Hang on, Jasp! I'm not finished!" He looked at Leana who was now eyeing both of them suspiciously.

Jonathon wasn't sure how to explain the next part without sounding like an idiot, but he knew he had to. "I was so angry I took the liberty of reaching out and pinching Jasper's neck...to pay him back for something." He then looked at Leana for her reaction. He was aware the entire thing must sound ridiculous.

Leana still seemed guarded. "I am supposed to believe that?" She looked over at Jasper who then rubbed his neck. He hadn't yet caught on that she was thinking he'd been with another girl and only now began to make sense of what the bruise looked like. Jasper stepped toward Jonathon with both fists clinched.

"Dude! What are you doing? First you bring me a shake as a truce. Then you twist my neck…to make it look like a hickey? Then you take off and leave the dance…with MY girl!"

Leana's eyes widened at his reference, then gave Jasper a cautious look of endearment. "Did he really pinch your neck?" She stepped around Jonathon to take a closer look at Jasper's neck. "I thought…" She stopped, embarrassed to admit she had so quickly jumped to a conclusion.

"What?! No way, Leana!" He glared at Jonathon now. "Are you kidding me?! Is that what you were trying to make her think?" He didn't take his eyes off Jonathon as he questioned Leana. "I suppose he took you to his house to use his Machine, too!" Jonathon kept his eyes to the ground, unable to meet Jasper's piercing gaze.

Leana quickly interjected, "I didn't! I mean…what?" She turned to Jonathon. "Why would you do something to make me think Jasper has a hickey?" She looked back at Jasper for answers. "I am really lost here! Can you please tell me what is going on?"

Jonathon finally looked up. "I brought her over here, didn't I? I didn't hook her up to REMY." He looked at Leana and lied. "My machine. It's just a gimmick to get you to come over. It's nothing more than a machine to make you, or anyone who uses it, relax." He turned his head at an angle, so Leana couldn't see him winking at Jasper and held his breath. Thankfully, Jasper simply shook his head in disgust but said nothing.

"I'm sorry. I was mad at Jasper. But now I'm not and I want you two to make up." Jonathon dejectedly tried to apologize, hoping his best friend could forgive him.

The look on Leana's face gave away her astounded perception of the entire story. "Jon, I don't even know what to say. I can't believe you'd do such a thing…"

The three of them stood there quietly in the cool nighttime air as they let all that happened between them soak in. Jasper was staring at Leana, pleading with his eyes for her to believe what Jonathon was saying. Then Leana took a step toward Jasper. "I'm sorry I ever thought that about you." She reached out her arms and Jasper pulled her close. With Leana's head pressed into Jasper's chest in an embrace, Jasper motioned with a nod that it was okay and then tilted his head toward the street, letting Jonathon know it was time for him to leave.

Jonathon mouthed a thank you, then wasted no time skipping off as fast as his throbbing legs would let him. He wanted to get far away to avoid any chance of further conversation. His legs hobbled. In fact, his whole body ached, and he regretted not taking something for the pain earlier. He thought of the irony that the only muscle in his body not hurting was his heart. It should feel broken but he felt oddly at peace.

A good block away, he slowed his pace, allowing himself to reflect on the past few months. He really thought he wanted to be with Leana but, strangely, now he no longer cared. A sense of relief washed over him, thinking he may have just dodged a deep discord with his best friend.

Lost in thought and pondering what he should now do with REMY, Jonathon stopped when he approached the alley leading toward town. A tall figure was walking in his direction and Jonathon's heart anxiously sped up. He wondered if this person was the tall member from the gang he'd encountered before, though this person appeared heftier. When the figure emerged from the shadows and into the streetlight, Jonathon took a deep sigh of relief. It was JR, and for once, Jonathon was happy to see it was him.

"Whoa. You startled me. I thought you were…someone else!" Just then, it dawned on Jonathon that JR was alone and not with Kate. "Weren't you supposed to be with…" he hesitated, not wanting to give voice to his assumption.

"Sorry to scare you," JR chuckled. Jonathon didn't like the way JR made it sound, even if it was a true statement. "I was at work. Just heading to the dance."

Jonathon's mouth opened to speak but he paused, still processing what JR had just said. *So, where was Kate?* he thought. *She had said she was going to meet JR.* He carefully chose his words. "Did you…happen to see Kate tonight? I thought she mentioned she was going to see you."

JR looked at him as if he was stupid. "She came to relieve me at work, so I could go to the dance for a while. We split the shift." He put his hands out in a gesture, insinuating Jonathon's ignorance. JR then turned to leave, shaking his head. "See ya later!" he murmured, rolling his eyes.

Jonathon stood there for a moment. "Hey," he called out to JR. JR turned around but was still walking in a backward motion. "So…

you and Kate aren't...?" He left the question open ended, hoping JR would fill in the blank.

JR stopped. "Dating?" He started laughing loudly, making Jonathon feel foolish. "All she talks about is you, dude. She's a nice girl but...nah. She's all yours." He belted out one last laugh as he turned to leave.

Jonathon stood under the soft glow of the streetlight staring down the darkened road as JR walked off. He suddenly felt winded, like he had just finished a jog, and needed to take some deep breaths. His mind was spinning as he sought to make sense of the whole scenario. If JR was right about what he said, then Jonathon knew he only had himself to blame. If he hadn't allowed Kate to go up to his room and access REMY, she wouldn't be feeling this way. He closed his eyes as he lifted his head toward the sky. When he opened them, he looked straight up toward the light and noticed some sort of night bird, not quite as big as an owl, perched on top of the lamppost.

Still in a daze, Jonathon yelled out loud to his feathered audience. "So, what do YOU think about all of this?" The bird looked down but then immediately took off into the night. "You're a lot of help!" he hollered after it, watching the bird fly away. He lifted his hands to his head and dragged his fingers through his dark locks. Then he took off his glasses and rubbed his eyes as he started to walk. His legs were shouting for him to go home but something was telling him he needed to go see Kate. He felt a little sad that his carelessness might have caused a change in their relationship and worried what she might feel once she knew the truth.

According to JR, Kate would now be at the bookstore. He looked down the alley leading toward town. It pained him to think of adding unnecessary steps but decided he preferred the well-lit streets and chose the slightly longer route.

Glad that the bookstore didn't close for about another half hour, Jonathon walked at a snail's pace. He was thinking about all the years he and Kate had been friends and about how she had recently become moody and was acting weird at times. Then he thought about the dream she said she had but wouldn't reveal to him. He turned the corner onto the main street of town and caught himself smiling, knowing JR wasn't seeing Kate as anything more than a friend.

Killing a little time, Jonathon found a bench a few blocks away from Juniper Books and plopped down with a sigh. Several kids lined the street, many he recognized who had been at the dance earlier. He sat with his elbows resting on his knees and his head in his hands looking at the ground. Feeling excitement growing at the chance to talk to Kate, he also felt a little nervous. He had always been able to talk to her in the past about anything. At least, anything up until the time he had started noticing Leana. He briefly looked up, surprised to see his parents strolling toward him about a block away, hand in hand, laughing and talking, each with an ice cream cone in their opposite hands. Jonathon straightened up and stood when they approached with their bewildered faces. His whole body felt so miserably stiff and sore that he squirmed and twisted just to be able to take a step.

"Jon! What are you doing downtown? We thought you were at the school dance." His mom came toward him to lean in for a hug. Even though she only gave a soft squeeze, he winced a little from his ailing muscles.

"Are you okay?" His dad chimed in with the same question.

"I was at the dance. It was pretty cool. But I just came down to…um…see someone." He felt the blood rush to his face, although he doubted they could tell from under the dim streetlight. Their eyes were questioning, so he satisfied their curiosity. "Um…just Kate." His parents knew her well and they nodded approvingly.

Then his mom gave him a sly grin as she cocked her head to one side. "Well…okay." She reached over and grabbed his father's hand. "We were just out for a little walk and decided to get an ice cream. We'll leave you alone to go…" She turned to look down the street. "…meet up with Kate. Plan on dinner at home tomorrow, will you? We didn't even see you last night when you came home." She gave a flirty smile to her husband but then looked back at her son. "Things have been a little hectic and we haven't had much family time lately. Oh…and if you'd like to invite Kate, we'd love to have her…"

Kate had been a guest at his house numerous times but this invitation seemed different. "I'll be there." He hesitated a moment. "I'll have to let you know about Kate tomorrow morning."

As his parents left, he rejoiced watching them walk away. Certainly, he had REMY to thank for their renewed closeness. It was still just so amazing to him, the impact of a simple dream, or perhaps multiple dreams. He'd likely never know for sure what those dreams were. As he began walking toward the bookstore, he again wondered what Kate had dreamt.

When he reached Juniper Books, he peered from the dark night outside into the well-lit bookstore. He saw only a few kids walking around the aisles, chatting, and laughing in small groups. Nestled on giant floor pillows in the Children's section near the front window, a mother was reading a book to two young children.

At first, he saw no sign of Kate but within a few seconds she emerged through a back door lugging a small stack of books and heaved them onto a counter. She was still wearing the dress she wore to the dance but had slipped her logo imprinted work apron over it. He felt proud of her as he watched her sifting through some pages and scribbling notes on a notepad next to the cash register. He gazed at her warmly, admiring the delicate way she was holding her pen and taking care of business so confidently.

Suddenly, as if sensing she was being watched, she stopped what she was doing and lifted her head, looking straight out the window toward Jonathon. Her mouth fell slightly open when she saw him. She hesitated but then quickly scanned the store. When no customers seemed to need her assistance, she left the check-out register and briskly walked down an aisle toward the front of the store.

When she opened the front door, the little bells attached to its handle jingled. Keeping the door ajar with her body, she stood with her mouth still open. Jonathon was standing with his hands in his pockets at a loss for words. "Hi," was all that came out of his mouth.

"What are you doing here, Jon? I thought you'd still be at the dance." She spoke in a hushed tone, then quickly glanced back into the store. When she realized no one was paying attention to her, she turned toward him again.

"Um..." He cleared his throat causing her to furrow her brow in anticipation. "Um..." *Just say something,* he told himself. "I just want to talk to you...I mean...once you get off work." He didn't usually have a hard time looking her in the eyes but tonight her mesmerizing gaze was making him feel uncomfortable.

Kate looked around behind her again and then stepped outside, leaving one heel behind her to keep the door cracked open. "I will be off in about ten minutes. You're making me nervous. What's wrong?"

He put both of his hands on her shoulders and noticed them relax a little under his touch. "Don't worry, Kate. I'll see you in 10 minutes." He turned her around, still holding her shoulders and gave her a gentle nudge while reaching over her head to push the door back open. She walked inside, looking over one shoulder at him with a guarded look, still furrowing her brow as she headed back to the register where some students were starting to line up.

Jonathon decided to go next door to The Coffee Couch for something warm to drink. The place was more crowded than usual, mostly kids congregating after the dance. He waited in line nearly ten minutes before ordering a couple of extra-hot mocha drinks, knowing they would rapidly cool down in the cold evening air. In his head, he tried rehearsing what he wanted to say to Kate but the noisy crowds kept distracting him. Besides, he really didn't know what he should say. Just that morning he was longing for Leana's attention but in the past few hours those feelings had deteriorated. He wondered if his feelings started to change before this evening but his ambitious pursuit to make REMY a success pushed his true feelings aside. Oddly, he now felt genuinely happy for Leana and Jasper and quite relieved Leana never got around to using his Machine. *So, what SHOULD I tell Kate?* he questioned himself.

When the barista called his name, he grabbed the two drinks and headed outside. Looking down toward the bookstore, he saw Kate locking the front door and heading his way. She was bundled up in a navy-blue sweater that went down to her knees and had wrapped a knitted, powder blue scarf around her neck. As she approached Jonathon, he handed her one of the drinks.

"I'm glad I got you something hot. You're making me cold just looking at you."

Jonathon smiled to let her know he was teasing but Kate had a serious look on her face.

"I locked up a couple minutes early once the place cleared out, so no one could come in and make me late. Now, can you tell me what's up?" She put the cup to her mouth and blew inside before taking a sip.

Jonathon looked around. "Let's walk." He guided her down the street toward a corner park where there were fewer people. A small picket fence surrounded the grounds and they entered through a latched gate. The only other people in the park were a couple lying on a blanket, talking in the corner furthest from the street. Jonathon and Kate sat down next to each other at a picnic table near the deserted playground equipment.

Jonathon began to feel chilled now, but he knew it was partly due to nerves. Kate's sweater wrapped over her legs, and she kept her hands cupped around the mocha for warmth. She was looking at the ground when she began to speak, but Jonathon started to say something at the same time. They both stopped and laughed for a second, helping him relax.

"OK. Me first," Jonathon demanded. He looked at her face searching for permission. She sat quietly waiting, so he continued. "We've known each other for a really long time, haven't we?" It came off more like a statement than a question, but Kate smiled and nodded her head to answer anyway.

"Go on…" She took another sip of her mocha, allowing Jonathon time to continue.

"I have been a little worried lately…" This statement made Kate lift her face toward his with a concerned look.

"Worried? About what?" Her eyes glistened under the street-light much like they had in the pseudo park setting of the dance.

Jonathon cleared his throat, and then cautiously continued. "You, actually."

Kate's lips parted slightly in response and though she looked like she wanted to say something, nothing came out.

"I wasn't sure what was going on between you and JR…" he continued.

"JR?" She paused. "Nothing is going on. What do you mean? And...why would that concern you?" She tilted her head now with a look of anticipation as she waited for his reply.

"It's just...I know he and Leana just broke up and I didn't want you to get hurt. You know...like if he was on the rebound..."

Kate stood up and turned to look down at Jonathon who was still seated. "Why would you worry about that?" She was standing so close to him, the steam coming out of her hot drink began fogging his glasses. When he reached up and took them off, Kate had a surprised look on her face. She started chuckling. "I don't remember the last time I've seen you without your glasses!"

Jonathon cleaned them off with his sleeve before putting them back on. "I couldn't see." He pointed to her drink.

"Sorry." She switched her mocha to her opposite hand and turned slightly away.

"I...didn't mean that in a bad way." A slight breeze blew between them as they stared at each other long enough to let it calm down. Kate broke the silence with a hushed plea. "Please, go on. I'm very interested in hearing why you were...concerned."

Jonathon felt his body starting to shiver as he grew more tense about the conversation. Kate noticed him shivering. "I feel so bad. You need a warmer jacket."

"It's okay. I think I'm just..." He stopped himself, momentarily feeling he could pass out from his nerves. "I have to tell you about something," Jonathon blurted out, feeling he needed to just get it over with. Kate didn't even flinch at his comment, so he knew he couldn't stop now. "You know those dreams you had? I think they're REMY's fault."

Kate set her drink on the picnic table and tightened the sweater around her body with her folded arms. She looked down at the ground instead of toward Jonathon. "I don't know who REMY is, but I've had way more than the two dreams I've told you about, Jon." Jonathon was staring up at Kate with a stupefied expression. "They started…maybe last year." She rushed out those last three words so quickly Jonathon had to slow them down in his mind to process what she was saying.

"You mean, the day after you came to my house, the day Leana was there…that wasn't your first dream…about…me?" He slowed his question, so he could carefully choose his words, making sure he understood her correctly.

Kate sat back down on the bench and looked down at her feet as she spoke. "Why would you think I liked JR? I've tried not to show it but…" She looked at Jonathon and her eyes were glossy. He thought she was about to cry. "I only think about you," she admitted. She began biting her lower lip, looking back down at the ground.

Jonathon was stunned by her admission. Even though JR had said as much, Jonathon thought Kate was only dreaming about him because REMY had helped her to dream about him. And now, here she was telling him her feelings, which apparently had been there long before that day he found her in his room with the headphones on. Thinking about it, he realized there really had been little chance Kate could have had enough time on his machine for it to have had much of an impact. And if that was true, Jonathon had nothing to feel guilty about.

He reached for her hand, causing her to look up at him again. Her soft features looked so delicate and vulnerable, surprising Jonathon with a tidal wave of emotion. Hardly even realizing what he was doing, he leaned forward and gave Kate a slow, soft kiss on her lips. When he backed away slightly, Kate was now the one who looked to be frozen. Her eyes remained closed, and her lips were still slightly puckered. Gradually opening her eyes, she gave Jonathon a shy grin showing off her dimples. Then she quickly jolted forward to give him another quick kiss on the lips, causing them to bump foreheads.

They both laughed as she apologized. "Sorry. I wasn't expecting that…I mean the kiss, not the head bump. Well, actually, not that either," she said shyly and giggled. "Neither was I, Kate." And then he turned to lift his leg over the bench, straddling the seat to face her. He pulled her into his arms and rubbed her back as if to keep her warm and then he kissed the top of her head. This was different than any feeling he had felt about Leana. An excitement, yet so comfortable.

With the side of her face pressed gently and warm against Jonathon's chest, Kate whispered. "So, do you want to tell me who REMY is? Why do you think it's someone else's fault for how I feel?"

Jonathon squeezed Kate a little tighter and smiled to himself. "Never mind. It's nothing important. REMY is just a project of mine that I don't think I ever needed." He then lifted Kate's chin with his hand and kissed her again, just like he'd seen in the movies.

The following morning, Jonathon gradually opened his eyes as a sliver of sunlight channeled its way through the window shutters that weren't completely closed, landing smack on his face. He lifted his covers to block the intruding glow and as he stretched his arms and legs out to wake up his body; he found himself smiling as he recalled the previous evening.

After walking Kate to her house and sealing the long day with another kiss, he made his way home and quietly snuck in without his parents hearing him. By only the light of the television, he spotted them snuggled together on the living room sofa watching a movie. He didn't want to disturb their happy place, and besides, he was exhausted from the long day and had little energy left to brief them. Instead, he tiptoed into the kitchen, wrote a note telling them he was home safe and left it on the counter in case they later became worried he was still out. As he crept his way up to bed, he decided he wouldn't program another dream tonight. *Maybe never*, he thought. His head hit his pillow and before he drifted off, he laid still in the dark wondering if REMY had really done all it seemed. There was no other way (that Jonathon was aware of) to explain what was happening between his parents. And REMY certainly seemed to have influenced Jasper, though the outcome wasn't what Jonathon had originally planned. Then there was Lulu. How she had reacted to Mr. Mercado was too crazy to write off as a fluke.

Shifting his thoughts back to his original goal when he built REMY, Jonathon wondered if he would have ever had dreams of Leana without the help of his Machine.

Because now, in one short day, his feelings for Leana had completely shifted to Kate. And he had just woken from an awesome dream about Kate without any help from his Machine. He smiled, thinking he couldn't wait to spend the day with her…and if what she said was true, her feelings had nothing to do with REMY either.

He hadn't yet decided but it was likely he would soon dismantle his brilliant invention to avoid any further anguish or wasted time. He sat up in bed just as he heard a ping from his phone. He reached for his desk to pick it up and saw a missed call from an unknown number. Jonathon sat up to play back the voicemail.

Hey, Jon. It's Sol. I ran into your housekeeper last night. Can you believe that she recognized me? (laugh) Anyway, she gave me your number. She seemed really happy with Mr. Mercado and so I told her my dad has a new girlfriend who is really cool but…you know, he kinda has cold feet. So, ya, she said something about you having a friend named REMY that could help, and I should call you. Not sure who that is but Lulu seemed pretty excited, so, ya. Call me. Maybe we can hang out one day and you can tell me about your friend REMY. K. Later

Jonathon lay back on his bed and couldn't help but laugh out loud. Then he looked over at REMY proudly perched on his desk and addressed his machine as if it could hear him. "I guess our adventures together might not yet be over, my friend." Jonathon wasn't sure how he could help Sol's dad but he knew if REMY helped with others, there was always a possibility.

After all his months of planning and thinking he wanted Leana, Kate had been right there in front of Jonathon the whole time. He smiled. He knew Jasper was happy now and Jonathon felt confident their strong friendship would allow Jasper to eventually forgive him. *Even though what I did to him was pretty awful,* he thought. He picked up the phone to call Kate, and as he did, he recalled Lulu saying there was always a rainbow after the storm. And as usual, it looked like she was going to be right.

Acknowledgements

First, I must give credit to my daughter Lauren who helped me come up with the idea and the name of REMY. She designed the book cover and politely answered my numerous texts and calls for feedback, suggestions, and help with technology along the way. I couldn't have come this far without her help.

My desire for writing began when I was in search of reading material for my young teen and pre-teen boys, Greg and Michael. I thank them for inspiration and insight into the life and minds of boys coming of age, though they bear little resemblance to Remy's main character, Jonathon.

And for my husband, Marvin, who has not skipped a beat in his support and encouragement throughout every step; thank you from the bottom of my heart.

Others I would like to acknowledge are friends and family who took the time to read first drafts to nearly final drafts; Lauren, Marvin, Brenda A., Charlene, Rhonda, Laura, Susy…you know who you are, and I appreciate you all so much.

About The Author

D.K. Posner grew up in California and Oregon and currently resides in Southern California with her husband. Her greatest joy in life is being with her family. She has had a long career as a Registered Nurse. Besides writing, she is very active and has many hobbies including golf, travel and getting together with friends.